Pelican Books
Mind Specials
Depression
Ross Mitchell

Ross Mitchell studied medicine at Edinburgh University and psychiatry
at St Francis Hospital, Haywards Heath. He was a psychiatrist with the
R.A.M.C., and at Barrow Gurney Hospital, Bristol. He is currently
Consultant Psychiatrist to Fulbourn and Addenbrooke's Hospitals,
Cambridge. He is particularly interested in community psychiatry and
works directly with general practitioners, nurses and social workers in
Health Centres. Dr Mitchell is married with two children.

His book *Phobias* is also published in Penguin.

MIND (National Association for Mental Health) is a charity
concerned with the needs of the mentally ill and handicapped,
and with the promotion of mental health. It draws attention
to inadequacies in the health service and campaigns for better
standards of care. It runs homes, schools and hostels as well
as advisory services, courses, conferences and a public
information department. It has over one hundred and thirty-five
active local groups who are concerned with alleviating mental
stress in the community.

MIND, 22 Harley Street, London W1N 2ED. Tel: 01 637 0741.
MIND OFFICE IN WALES, 7 St Mary Street, Cardiff CF1 2AT.
Tel: 0222 395 123
MIND NORTHERN REGIONAL OFFICE, 4 Park Lane, High Street,
Gateshead, Tyne and Wear NE8 3LZ
MIND YORKSHIRE REGIONAL OFFICE, 155–7 Woodhouse Lane,
Leeds LS2 3EF. Tel: 0532 453 926

ROSS MITCHELL

Penguin Books
in association with MIND

DEPRESSION

Penguin Books Ltd, Harmondsworth, Middlesex, England
Penguin Books, 625 Madison Avenue, New York, New York 10022, U.S.A.
Penguin Books Australia Ltd, Ringwood, Victoria, Australia
Penguin Books Canada Ltd, 2801 John Street, Markham, Ontario, Canada L3R 1B4
Penguin Books (N.Z.) Ltd, 182-190 Wairau Road, Auckland 10, New Zealand

First published 1975
Reprinted 1975, 1976, 1977, 1979, 1981, 1983

Made and printed in Great Britain by
Fletcher & Son Ltd, Norwich

Set in IBM Univers by Herts Typesetting Services Ltd, Hertford

Illustration acknowledgements

Pages 7, 12, 76–7 to Chris Schwarz; page 13 to Tony Othen;
pages 24, 25 (right) to Nick Hedges; page 32 (top) to Jean Mohr;
pages 40–41 to John Cavanagh; page 72 to Angela Phillips; page 90
to John Walmesley; pages 94–5 to Mark Edwards; page 83 to
Janine Wiedel; page 91 to the Samaritans; pages 11, 25 (left), 32
(bottom) to Camera Press; pages 64–8 to Euan Duff; pages 51–4
to *Punch*; pages 86–7 to the *Evening Standard*.

Contents

Introduction

Nearly everyone talks these days of being depressed, but what does 'being depressed' really mean? Is it a medical statement like 'being infected', or is it nearer the colloquialism 'being cheesed off'? When you use the word 'depression' what do you really mean? Can you describe it clearly in words that other people will understand? The chances are that you will find it very difficult to be precise, because the word 'depression' is used in so many different ways by different people.

To some, depression is a mood, to others it is a particular kind of experience. To others again it may mean a particular attitude to life, and to some depression is an illness. All these things are loosely called depression, but what do we really mean by this word and what are the differences?

This is what this book is about; an attempt to penetrate beneath the imprecise words of everyday experience to discover the reality and substance underneath. This is not an easy task because we will have to try to think about the deeply felt responses which each of us has to the world around us. As human beings we are not machines with built-in, predictable responses to stimuli, we have a spirit as well — that part of our nature which makes each of us unique individuals. It is in this world of the spirit that depression, whatever its nature and whatever its cause, is experienced, and it is into this world of the spirit that we now have to venture.

I am particularly indebted to John Payne of the National Association for Mental Health for suggesting the initial content and layout of this book, and for giving me personal encouragement in the early stages of its writing.

CHAPTER 1
THE NATURE OF DEPRESSION

Depression as a mood

We all like to think of ourselves as even-tempered people; well-balanced, equable in all things and well in control of ourselves. This gives rise to the incorrect belief that our day-to-day mood is constant — that we keep to an even emotional tenor in all our ways. This is not so.

Our feelings follow a cyclical pattern — a little up, a little down; small variations from moment to moment, from hour to hour, from day to day. This follows the pattern of other bodily functions such as temperature and level of chemicals in the blood. This variability is based on what are known as circadian rhythms — twenty-four hour cycles of activity which are perhaps related to the alternation of the hours of light and the hours of darkness. As daylight comes and goes so does our 'mood'; the sum total of all our feelings at a given time. These feelings, the good and the bad, combine to give us a general feeling of well-being or of apprehension.

We talk colloquially of our mood going up and down. Depression happens when our mood is down. There are a number of slang phrases used to describe this feeling of 'downness': 'fed up', 'browned off', 'cheesed off', 'the downs', 'down in the dumps', 'the blues', 'the glooms', 'the miseries', 'feeling low', 'at a low ebb', 'lifeless', 'flat', and so on. Writers have also used words like 'melancholy' and 'anomie'. Melancholy harks back to an old theory that our mood was determined by the amount of a given fluid (or 'humour') in the body and people sometimes still talk of being 'out of humour'. In melancholy there was thought to be an excess of black bile (**melas khole** in Greek) in the body. Anomie implies a lack of energy or vital spirit in a person.

The word depression, when applied to a state of mood, shares with all these colloquial words and phrases a sense of being down in spirit, low in energy, having a sense of loss, hopelessness and uselessness. It implies apathy and pessimism. The opposite mood would be typified by enthusiasm, joy, hopefulness and optimism.

A depressed mood very often comes on after disappointment, or a sense of having lost something, but often it can come out of the blue, apparently spontaneously. Some people are more prone to this apparently spontaneous shift of mood and are said to be cyclothymic. I say apparently spontaneous because clinical experience with patients shows that there is nearly always a preceding cause for a mood change, but the person experiencing it is not always aware of the cause. As the person talks with the doctor, he will become aware of events that have, as it were, triggered off the mood change. A few patients vigorously deny this, but they can be shown to be avoiding a situation or occurrence which has been particularly painful or embarrassing to them.

In this sense of having a depressed mood, we all get depressed. It can occur on its own, but is often accompanied by another feeling — anxiety. This is an unpleasant feeling of anticipated disturbance. The very fact of becoming depressed, of itself, can spark off anxiety in susceptible people; in others, depression arises in conjunction with anxiety or is initiated by it.

Depression as an experience

Moods arise out of all kinds of experiences. An experience inevitably linked to a depressed mood is that of feeling devalued and losing a sense of being appreciated, or being loved as a person. This sense of loss itself is often called depression, as well as the mood of depression to which the feeling of loss can lead.

As well as a **depressed** mood, this experience of losing something valuable can be associated with feelings of frustration and resentment. When we are depressed we often want to be quiet and keep to ourselves: when we are frustrated or resentful we want to attack the object of our frustration and resentment. A mixture of depression with anxiety, frustration and resentment are the ingredients of a very disturbing state called agitation. Obviously it disturbs the person suffering from it and it also disturbs those who see that the person is agitated — like many extreme moods, aspects of this experience are socially infectious.

Depression as an attitude to life

The concept of 'temperament' is used to describe types of people and separate them into contrasting groups: warm-hearted, cold-hearted; stable, unstable; confident, diffident; optimistic, pessimistic. These are descriptions of a continuing aspect of personality rather than a passing emotional response. Our temperament can be thought of as a measure of our customary general attitude to life and its fortunes.

People can be divided roughly into those who cope with life and those who do not — like all generalizations this is true only in the widest sense. Most people can cope with **some** things but **not** with others, but there are people who are generally 'inadequate' and have to rely on others for strength, encouragement and support. Some of these people are chronically pessimistic; they expect the worst out of life and usually get it. Rabindranath Tagore, the great Indian philosopher, said, 'Expect nothing and then you will not be disappointed'. This is the attitude of the cynic or, perhaps, the sceptical realist. The attitude of the depressed personality is 'There is no use hoping for anything; I always get the worst that's going'. It is important to distinguish the **transient**

pessimism, which is part of the depressed mood, and the
persistent pessimistic attitude which is part of the depressed
personality. The first is a response to a stimulus; the second is
an attitude to life.

Depression as an illness

Moods, experiences and attitudes can be common to any of us.
They may not make us happy, but they do not necessarily
mean that we are sick; they just show how we happen to be at a
given time, whereas illness implies a discontinuity, a change from
health into sickness. At one moment a person is fit and well,
functioning pretty satisfactorily, then suddenly he is sick; he
has become a patient who feels distressed, loses his
effectiveness, and shows disturbance of his bodily and mental
functions. He is 'no longer himself' as we put it. It is not
always easy to be sure when somebody is actually ill. Some
moods can be so severe and incapacitating that they merge
into illness. It is not necessarily a matter of severity even, but
of a person's ability to absorb stress and deal with it. Illness
implies that the machine has broken down in some way. For
example, computers have a built-in mechanism which switches
them off when they are being overloaded; it is a protective

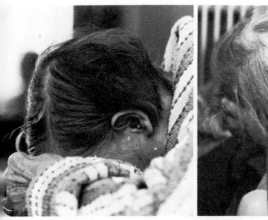

device. Depression can be thought of in the same way — a protective mood, which temporarily switches the person off until he can cope better. If the computer cut-out does not work in time, or fails, the machine will blow a fuse and stop until the faulty part is replaced. Depressive illness, as opposed to depressive mood, is like that, the machine has gone wrong; it needs **help** to be put right again.

The word 'depression' can be deceptively simple. When we talk to each other we must define what we mean by depression. Otherwise when one of us means mood, another may mean illness; when one of us is talking about experience, another may mean attitude to life. As we go on to look further into the nature of depression in all its different aspects, these basic distinctions and definitions should be kept in mind.

CHAPTER 2
CAN DEPRESSION EVER BE NORMAL?

If we accept that depression is a common human experience, we have to ask if the experience is normal or not. The answer has important practical consequences. If the depression is considered abnormal, there is the implication that something ought to be done about it. Whether something **can** be done or not is yet another question, but abnormality as such implies an undesirable state. If the depression is judged to be normal, it may well have a therapeutic or healing effect, in which case, not only is there nothing abnormal to 'treat', but also intervention may deprive the individual of a valuable experience by suppressing the depression with drugs or other physical treatments. We are assuming in this argument that all depression is not necessarily abnormal. This is based on concepts of normality which we should examine before going any further.

The word 'normal' has four basic meanings in common usage: something that is **statistically common** and occurs frequently; something that is **customary** in given circumstances; something that is **appropriate** to given circumstances and something that is **desirable** to the group. This means that we can only understand 'normality' in reference to the group: the society around us of which we are a part. 'Normality' is a judgement of the behaviour or experience of one person, compared to the group from which he comes. Let us now look at each meaning of normality in turn in relation to depression.

Statistically common

'Most people are normally depressed after a disappointment.' This is a statement based on observation — the majority of people, in given circumstances, behave in this way, it is an aspect of average behaviour. The more a person's behaviour approximates to the average or norm of his group, the more 'normal', in this sense, is his behaviour.

Customary

'It is normal for depressed people to want to be by themselves.' This is a statement about expectation and about what is acceptable. It reflects what has come to be accepted as customary by common consent in the group. It is not just an observation, it also implies a value judgement about people in general.

Appropriate

'I think he had every right to be depressed when he lost his job. His depression was normal.' This is now a value judgement about an individual's behaviour; he is showing what is common and customary and, in addition, his behaviour is felt to be **appropriate** to his circumstances.

Desirable

'I do not think it's normal for her to be depressed all the time.' Here there is the implication that something is not only inappropriate, but also undesirable. Remember, however, that behaviour may be appropriate without (at the same time) being desirable. The statement also implies that something ought to be done, because the behaviour is considered to be undesirable by the group.

Looking at concepts of normality also involves giving some thought to concepts of deviance. Deviance is a measure of distance from the group norm. The more deviant behaviour is held to be, the further away it is from what is felt to be normal or average. Normality is usually a static judgement — a thing is either normal or it is not — whereas deviance is a dynamic judgement. Deviance can vary in degree from time to time. But even normality is relative; standards of normality in any culture change and develop but, within this changing pattern a particular piece of behaviour can be measured for its deviance from the current norm.

Is deviance synonymous with abnormality and sickness? The more deviant behaviour becomes, the more abnormal it is thought to be, but to be abnormal is not necessarily to be sick or ill. Illness is defined in our society by group consent, and it exists when abnormality has passed beyond certain limits. Look, for example, at heights: in this country the average adult

man is 1·78 metres tall; to be under 1·52 metres or over 1·83
metres is unusual but not abnormal; to be under 1·37 metres
or over 1·98 metres would be abnormal but not necessarily
evidence of sickness; to be under 1·21 metres or over 1·99
metres would be highly abnormal and might well be evidence
of some underlying illness. Even so, the person concerned
might not feel ill.

Illness

This carries within it ideas of disease in the sense of discomfort.
If we look at most accepted illnesses, whether they are physical
or psychological in origin, we usually find: **a disturbance** in the
individual's normal physical or psychological functioning; **a
disfunction** — the individual is no longer as efficient as usual;
and **distress** — either of the individual in that he feels upset, or
of others around him, in that he upsets them in some way.
Illness also implies a 'discontinuity' in health. The individual
was healthy; now he is ill. This sounds simple, but we can get
into great difficulties if we try to define health; like normality
it is a value judgement. It is useful to look at what goes to
make up the illness we have now diagnosed. It is made up of
two components: the direct result of the disturbance, which
we might call strain, and the body's defence mechanisms
brought into action to minimize the effects of that strain.

Fever is a good example of this illness model: following an
infection, inflammation is caused in a part of the body. This
inflammation causes symptoms of strain which are reflected
in fever, but the fever also mobilizes the body's defence

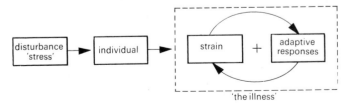

Stress on the individual leads to strain plus response which
together constitute illness

mechanisms such as an increase in white cells and antibodies which combat the infecting organism. So 'the illness' of the fever is both strain and response.

Depression can be thought of in just the same way. The actual symptoms and signs of depressive illness can be **both** the result of strain on the individual, as we have described, **and** also the individual's psychic defence mechanisms mobilized to make an adaptation in the face of that strain.

Certain words used in the context of illness need defining. **Symptoms** are what the **patient** (the person who is judged to be ill) experiences; whereas **signs** are what other people (usually doctors, nurses, social workers, friends and relatives) see in the patient. Symptoms are subjective; signs are objective. Symptoms and signs are grouped together in commonly occurring associations known as **syndromes**. When a syndrome occurs again and again with recognizable cause, and can be clearly diagnosed separately from other syndromes, and has a specific treatment and **prognosis** (outlook), it is classified as an **illness**. When symptoms and signs are present but a basic cause is uncertain or unproved, but the person is still distressed and disturbed, the word **disordered** is commonly used.

So, we can summarize our assessment of a given 'depression' in a given individual, remembering that within the word 'depression' is covered mood, experience, attitude or illness.

The summary diagram (p. 19) implies that what starts as a normal response can, in given circumstances, be pushed into an abnormal one, leading either to ultimate depressive disorder or depressive illness.

What, then, is meant by 'normal' depression in the sense of potential healing? Depression as an experience can have a protective aspect. This can come about in four ways:

Depression can **lower responsiveness** so that a depressed person does not respond too violently to the stress around him. As the stress increases, the resulting depression acts as a reciprocal protective screen.

If the external stress becomes too great, the depression can act as a **cut-out**: the person stops responding altogether. This has its drawbacks, because it also stops any adaptive responses

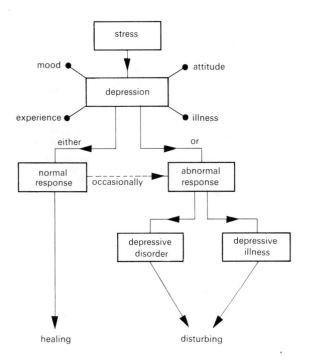

Stress leading to depression, which then expresses itself either as a normal depression (potentially healing), or as an abnormal depression (potentially disordering). An abnormal depression is divided into depressive disorder and depressive illness

taking place but, presumably, the cut-out is activated when basic survival is threatened — adaptation can come later.

With its associated grief and weeping, depression has a **cathartic effect** — pent-up emotions are expressed, the cork is blown out of the bottle, and adaption — which otherwise might be inhibited by the unexpressed feelings can then begin.

Finally, depression can be thought of as a period of time during which the individual diverts his energies inwards while he is making an adaptation to external events. He is pulling up the drawbridge — not just to keep the enemy out, but so that he can spend time getting his defensive guns ready.

CHAPTER 3
DEPRESSION AND EARLY INFANCY

Links between experience in early childhood and how we behave later as adults are pretty well established. For example, for some people, losing a parent at a critical age in childhood results in depression later in life.

Psychoanalysts — specialists in making an analysis of the experiences of people in terms of their relationships with others — have always been interested in the very earliest experiences of life. They have focused their attention on the mother—infant relationship and have discovered that depression may have its roots in the very earliest interactions between the mother and her newly born baby. This may sound quite fanciful, but it does have very practical consequences for us, not only in understanding how depression comes about, but also in setting up programmes of treatment. Mother and baby together are a functional unit each dependent upon the other; although the baby is obviously the more dependent of the two, the mother depends on the baby in the sense that the baby evokes her maternal feelings. Security for both grows out of this interdependence. With this basis of security established, learning takes place — the mother learns to respond effectively to her child's needs, the child learns gradually to become an autonomous individual, who literally learns to stand on his own feet.

In the world as the child experiences it, he 'sees' the mother as part of himself — that part representing contentment, peace, happiness and safety. Only later can he distinguish 'me' and 'not me' — 'this mouth is part of me, but that breast is part of her'.

In the beginning then, child and mother are one and the same, and this gives rise to a very basic feeling that 'all's well with the world', so much so, that much of subsequent human behaviour appears to be devoted to trying to recreate this type of closeness.

Within this reciprocal, functional unit the mother's role is to meet the demands of the baby, and it is the repeated, predictable meeting of demands that builds up what Erik Erikson, a psychoanalyst, calls **basic trust**. Mother's giving, feeding breast becomes the 'good breast' because it is always there, always available, always satisfying for the baby.

The terrible day must come when the breast does not appear on demand, and this is a very traumatic moment in the child's development. Suddenly that part of the unit which means safety to him is not there, and there is, however dimly perceived it may be by him, a sense of loss which brings pain, anxiety and fear. The baby may suck on his fingers as a substitute, but in the process he swallows air which causes his stomach to swell which aggravates his distress by being painful. There is no one there to help him bring up his wind and so the 'loss' of his mother becomes synonymous with pain and distress.

Once the baby is able to see his mother as a separate individual, he can begin to try to control her so that she will not go away. He can cry, and see if she comes to investigate; he can hide under the blanket (she has gone) and peep out again (she has come back); he can drop things out of his cot and see if she comes to pick them up for him.

All of this behaviour can be interpreted as the baby learning, in a primitive way, to gain control over his mother to ensure that she will not ever leave him again. Even so, his mother cannot always be around, nor may she even want to be, and the baby has to come to terms with the fact that his mother **will** go away at times.

So long as he learns the second lesson — that she will ultimately return — **basic mistrust** can be avoided. Time scales are very important in this context; a baby's demand is immediate; he cannot bear to wait. What to his mother is only a few minutes is an eternity to the baby. Nevertheless, if she ultimately does come back in reasonable time, the baby learns to postpone his gratifications.

By this time, the stage of what analysts call 'object relations' has been reached. The child lives in a world surrounded by objects (including people) and he feels, in an omnipotent way, that all objects (and hence other people) are there to serve him. Some of his objects are more prized than others. His mother comes first, often followed by some object used as a substitute for mother when she is not there. We have all had a first teddy-bear, or a blanket, which, no matter how tattered it becomes, was held on to tenaciously and gave comfort when mother was not there.

Objects which give comfort and reassurance and can be relied upon are **good objects** (loved objects) whereas those which are learned to be unreliable and even give pain, are seen as **bad objects**. Parts of the child himself can almost be treated as bad objects; for example, his teeth when they give him pain in the teething stage. He perceives 'a badness which is inside me'. In turn, the child can become angry and bite, becoming what is known as orally aggressive (sadistic in that he may want to hurt something outside himself). **Or** he may turn to himself for comfort, almost learning to 'enjoy' his pain when there is no other relief, what is called masochistic in other contexts (an enjoyment of hurting oneself).

All this self-discovery and learning process has a relationship to depression in that it is now thought that the early loss of a loved object is the basis of all subsequent depression. The **anticipation** of losing a loved object gives rise to anxiety; the **actual** loss of the object gives rise to depression. Thus depression and anxiety are very closely linked to each other.

Depression in later life recapitulates much of this early experience. There is a sense of loss leading to inner emptiness; there is anger and resentment turned outwards; the anger may be orally 'biting' — the sarcastic tongue and the resentful voice; there is pain turned inwards. There can be a sense of badness projected outwards towards others ('It's all their fault') or turned inwards ('It's all my fault, I am to blame, I am unworthy'), or there can be a return to oral satisfaction — over-eating, excessive drinking, reliance on drugs.

All people experience 'loss' of their mothers by this process, but not all become depressives. Why is this? The answer depends on timing and intensity. Losing a loved object at particularly important stages of our development is more damaging than at others: for example, René Spitz, a research worker, examined a number of deprived children and discovered that they had 'lost' their mothers by being separated from them between six and eight months of age and were depressed as a result. If the separation lasted longer than three months their depression was more marked and less reversible, the children showed signs of apathy, dejection and isolation. This kind of depression results directly from the loss of an important person upon whom the child was leaning.

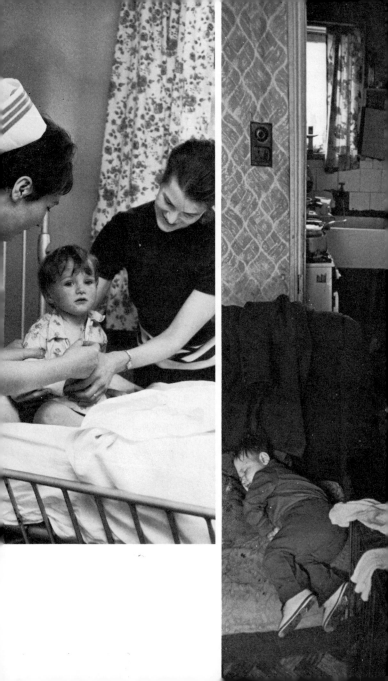

At an earlier stage of development, in the first weeks of life, it has been shown that if a child is given plenty of nourishment but no handling he may cease to thrive, and in the extreme case may die. Firm, comforting handling is vital in the early mother—child relationship and if it is absent, it constitutes a loss which may lead not only to depression but also to death. So, it is not only the **amount** of the loss and the **quality** of the loss, but its **timing** that is important in creating a person who may become a depressive in later life.

Having emphasized loss through separation, an important concept related to depression called **separation anxiety** needs explaining. It is a stage once removed from actual loss. As we have already seen, the child has to come to terms with the absence of his mother because she cannot always be there to answer all his needs. Mother is seen by him as a **security base**. This base becomes all the more important to older children when they have become mobile and are beginning to explore their world. Mother is someone safe to start out from, and someone safe to return to.

Watch a group of children and their mothers on the first day of a play group. Each child normally begins by sitting on mother's lap or firmly holding her hand. Having firstly buried his head in his mother's breast the child may tentatively reach out to touch an object or to **look** at the room. Exploration is beginning. There will be tentative forays but always a return to mother. Gradually confidence builds up as he explores further, gets down on the floor, walks a bit, before scurrying back. If he is finally reassured he may walk over to join a group of children who are playing with a pile of toys or a sand tray.

It is his mother's safeness, her being there for him, which ultimately lets him leave her and reach out to others. Of course she has to be secure enough to let him go; if she is too anxious for him, she may inhibit this exploratory drive and inadvertently tie him to her apron strings — an anxious child may often be the product of an anxious mother.

What happens if he goes out to explore, then wants to return to her and she is not there? Panic sets in, with severe **separation anxiety**. He may feverishly search round and round, calling out for her, trying to get back to his security base. If she cannot be found, he may suddenly freeze, turning inwards on himself, often in a corner with his back literally to the wall, or he may kick out at any stranger who comes near to comfort him. Freezing is a way of shutting out the world; if I keep still, perhaps the danger will go away, just as young rabbits freeze when the shadow of the sparrow-hawk passes over them. What does freezing achieve? It avoids danger ('Perhaps it will pass me by'). It avoids running into new danger ('I will stay here quiet by myself'). It avoids unpleasant thoughts ('I will not think about it or feel about it'). As we have said before, depression can also be seen as a kind of emotional freezing when the danger and pain of loss or separation are too much to tolerate.

A person who has experienced an excess of loss at a critical time in his development becomes not only more liable to depression in later life, but also at risk of developing a depressive personality. These are the people with a particular attitude to life which is depressive — the pessimists who can find no good in themselves, and precious little in others around them. They show two contrasting aspects of their personalities which are now easier to understand in terms of their reaction to this sense of basic loss.

Firstly, they are hungry for love and affection which they feel, rightly or wrongly, that they have missed. If they do not get enough, they show withdrawal effects and make great demands on others. They will swallow all that they can. They have a perpetually unsatisfied need to be loved, and constantly have to be reassured by others that they have some goodness in them. Secondly, they are chronically resentful, because they feel they are not loved or reassured enough and they have to find someone to blame. They feel bad inside themselves, and to get some relief from this they project this 'badness' on to others; 'It's your fault that I'm feeling the way I do. If only you had loved me enough, I wouldn't be like this now'.

The tragedy for the depressive personality is that in his demand for love and the way he goes about trying to get it, he drives away the very people from whom he might get something of what he is seeking. He will never get all that he is looking for, but he might just get enough to make life seem a little more tolerable for him, and make him a little more tolerable to others.

There are certain practical possibilities that arise which could be used to reduce the chances of people becoming depressed in later life. As far as mother—infant relationships are concerned, sensible mothering could go a long way to cutting down depression later. Children have to learn to cope with frustration; it would be unrealistic to suppose otherwise. What the mother can do is to make an effort to convey to her child the reality of her continuing love, which is not dependent on her continuing presence. This means teaching the child literally that 'no mother' does not equal 'no love'. The simple expedient of introducing mother substitutes, like the father or the grandmother, will help; taking care that the mother is not away from the child for long, unexpected periods will help too. If the child or mother have to be separated, perhaps by the need to go into hospital, the separation can be minimized by preparation where possible, and making provision for contact to be kept up as much as is realistic. This may mean reconsidering admitting mothers to hospitals with their babies, and reviewing the whole question of open visiting to children in hospitals.

The care of orphan children, and all children in institutions of whatever kind, such as day nurseries, foster homes, hospitals and schools, should be the subject of review and research. Children need to have physical contact and literally to be held and touched as much as they need shelter and three square meals a day. There is an unfortunate tendency nowadays to concentrate on physical welfare and to neglect or take for granted emotional and psychological welfare.

All of these practical suggestions lead to what Donald Winnicott, has called 'good enough mothering'; that is mothering which is realistic and good enough for the child's needs. So much of the early analytical work suggested that the child needed unconditional love, which is an idealized concept and certainly beyond the capabilities of human mothers, whoever they are.

We cannot prevent the experience of loss, but we can try to avoid such loss at critical times in development, and if we cannot, at least we should try to cut it down to the absolute minimum which is practically possible.

CHAPTER 4
DEPRESSION AND GRIEF

No one will deny that depression and mourning are closely connected. The person who is mourning is showing grief at his bereavement. **Bereavement** is the forcible loss of something that is precious, and is usually used in the context of the loss (death) of a person. **Grief** is the resulting emotional experience of being bereaved.

Most people would see grief as a natural response in the circumstances, and would be suspicious of someone who denied their grief, always showing the traditional 'stiff upper lip' attitude. Most people would also see grief as therapeutic, and people who have been bereaved are often advised to 'have a good cry and get it off your chest'. What people do not understand is that grief is an active process which involves hard work: it is not something passive such as letting out repressed feelings. It is an active process of adjustment and positive letting-go of someone who has been close to you. Gerald Caplan, a social psychiatrist, calls the process 'doing grief work'.

The importance of grief is that it is an intermediary phase between the experience of loss and some ultimate restitution. There are strong feelings to be dealt with which otherwise get in the way of the healing process. Depression is an important aspect of the grief reaction and is therefore involved in grief work.

Anticipatory stage

It is relatively rare for bereavement to come literally 'out of the blue'. Death is the one inescapable fact of our existence — 'In the midst of life we are in death'. We can live in expectation of death although this expectation may be largely unconscious and there is still shock when we are confronted with the reality of that anticipated in our imaginations. Even if the death comes at the end of a long illness, there is still the shock of the reality of the loss. If the death is sudden, because of a road accident for example, the shock is greater still.

Stage of loss

There is a feeling of emptiness — a space which once was filled by a person — something has been forcibly taken away. The loss is keen if the person was loved, but even if they were hated, there is still a loss — in this case a loss of the person who was the recipient of our bad and hostile feelings.

Stage of numbness

This is a primitive shutting-down, extreme depression of vital functions, the mechanical 'cut-out' which has been described already.

Stage of anger

If something is taken away from us we get angry, rebel and want to grab it back, we get indignant and wonder why it has happened to us. What have we done to deserve this? We feel prejudiced against, we want to be revenged and look round for someone to blame, someone accountable for our loss. This is a defence against the painful realization that it might be partly our fault that we have been bereaved.

Stage of searching

We set out to find that which is lost. This, in turn, is a denial that the object has gone for good. We keep looking, hoping to find it even if we know that we shall not in the end.

Stage of denial

When we do not find what is lost, we may deny to ourselves that we are **not** going to find it. 'It's just round the corner, I'll find it tomorrow, you wait and see. No, it's not gone, only hiding.' This is a kind of bizarre and desperate game we play with ourselves and with others. (These last three stages often alternate with each other: anger, searching, denial, searching, anger, and so on.)

Stage of acceptance

Gradually anger burns itself out; and searching ceases as the object is not found, denial subsides in the face of unavoidable reality.

Stage of letting-go

With the onset of acceptance the active stage of renunciation can begin, the letting-go of the lost object, the 'burial' of it in a psychological sense. A new life has to be created after the loss of the object, not enshrining it in its 'lostness', but letting it go and moving forwards into a new stage of living.

Stage of re-growth

This takes time, often with backward looks or even a return to previous stages. Ultimately, if the grief work has been done, re-growth will take place.

In reality these stages are not as neatly separated; they are blurred and merge into each other. The timing varies from person to person, circumstance to circumstance. The numbness may last a few moments, a few days, even a week; anger, searching and denial may go on for up to six months. Gradually acceptance, letting-go and re-growth take place in the second six months, so that by the first anniversary of the death, the grief process is being completed. There are often anniversary reactions, temporary renewals of the grief for a time, but they lessen in intensity as the years pass by.

Fifty-eight year old Mrs Thompson loses her husband. She is numb for a couple of days then begins to be angry, looking for someone to blame: 'If only we had . . . if only the doctor had . . .'. She searches for her husband — hears him upstairs, in the study, hears him putting the car away in the garage. She may even think that she has seen him for a fleeting moment in the street. She may deny that he is really dead, and may be tempted to go to seances to try to make contact with him again. Gradually she lets go and accepts, so that by the first anniversary of his death she is making better social contacts and beginning to live fully again. This is the pattern of normal grief.

Things often go wrong. Grief can be denied totally, or it can begin and then be inhibited. It may be internalized; turned inwards onto the body, instead of outwards into relationships. We may see on the surface a person who appears not to be affected by her grief, but her **bonhomie** is superficial, false and brittle. Behind the mask there is often a chronically depressed person who has not been able to begin grief work. If grief is delayed or inhibited, superficial relief is gained only temporarily. When grieving does start it is often more severe because of the delay. If the grief is denied altogether we get what is called pathological mourning and the person slips from grief, which is normal and healing, into depressive illness which is abnormal and distressing. When grief is turned inwards onto the body, the person will complain of ill-defined physical ailments. Murray Parkes who has done much research in the field has shown that, in the first six months after bereavement, widowers often complain of heart trouble and may literally die of a broken heart; and widows tend to consult their doctors with gastric upsets and rheumatic conditions.

It would be wrong to assume that there is a 'right' way to grieve. Custom and style vary from person to person, from culture to culture. Evelyn Waugh has written extensively about the American way of death, and Geoffrey Gorer, a social anthropologist, has recorded the widely different social rituals through which man has learnt to express his grief. There are many different ways to grieve: the point is not **how** it is done, but that it should be done somehow.

It is very easy to confuse the depression that is a part of grief with depression that is an illness. The bereaved person feels sad and lost; she cannot eat or sleep; she reproaches herself for not caring more for the lost one; she is much depressed and distressed. Kind friends may tell her not to cry, not to be so upset, to try to forget it all; that is what she must not do if she is to do her grief work. Family doctors may even be persuaded to prescribe drugs: sleeping pills, antidepressants and tranquillizers. If sleeplessness continues for more than three or four nights then perhaps a sleeping pill is justified, but antidepressants and tranquillizers only confuse the issue. There is **work** to be done, not an illness to treat. In fact, giving drugs at this time may inhibit grief and prompt an illness later. The bereaved person needs company and needs to be encouraged to talk about the dead person; she needs to cry if she wants to. She needs human support while she does her grief work, not human support to enable her to avoid it altogether.

Although we have chosen death as the example of bereavement, the concept is now being widened to include other losses such as the amputation of a limb or an abortion. What is lost here is a valued part of one's own body. Even the girl who does not want to be pregnant, grieves temporarily for the baby she has had to lose.

Then there is menopause and retirement. What is lost here is a certain status — a potential child-bearer, or a potential bread-winner; and finally, old age, where what is lost is a valued place in the family or in society itself. We must not think that we are only bereaved by death; we must grieve for these other aspects of our lives which are forcibly taken away from us too.

CHAPTER 5
DEPRESSION AND THE CRISES OF LIFE

Crisis is another of those words which we use without being
altogether aware of its essential meaning. When most of us talk
about a crisis, we are thinking about an emergency situation in
which something has to be done quickly to restore the **status
quo**. In its original sense, a crisis is a turning point in a
developmental pattern. The older physicians used to talk of
the 'crisis in pneumonia' as that time in the development of
the illness when the temperature was at its highest and could
then begin to fall, heralding the ultimate recovery of the
patient. Emotional crises are like this too. They represent
crucial points in a developmental history when the person can
either go on to further development and maturity, or can
regress to an earlier stage of growth. Gerald Caplan, previously
mentioned in connection with grief work, has studied
emotional crises, and has emphasized how important they are
for personal growth. He certainly sees them as emergencies,
but not necessarily something to be avoided; rather something
to be made use of for growth. In a sense, without our
emotional crises or turning points, we would not grow. Caplan
divides crises into two kinds: developmental crises which arise
at critical stages of emotional development; and adventitious
crises which can occur at any time in an individual's life
history, and which are concerned with events **around** rather
than within him.

Developmental crises occur whenever someone is about to
move from one stage of life history into another, or from one
role into another. There is the crisis of birth, the crisis of
becoming conscious of being a unique individual, the crisis of
self-discovery. These are followed by the crises of going to
school, having your first boy- or girl-friend, leaving school,
going to college or taking your first job, getting engaged,
getting married, having your first child and so on.

These crises reflect changes in degrees of dependency on
others as you move towards greater independence to a point at
which others become dependent upon you. They also reflect
changes in role, being an adolescent rather than a child, being a
student rather than a school pupil, becoming a teacher, a
fiancé, a husband or a father.

Adventitious crises arise in our relationship with outside
events which are potentially threatening to our ongoing

well-being or safety. These can be: **failures** which mean loss of material wealth or security; for example, failing exams, failing to get promotion, being declared redundant, being sacked, financial failures — either of our own making or of others which reflect on ourselves; **acute losses** which leave a painful space; for example, bereavement, abortion, infidelity, loss of a boy- or girl-friend, divorce, loss of sexuality, loss of efficiency as a result of severe illness or 'power failure'; or **cultural transitions** where there is a move, not only from one role to another, but also from one way of life to another with the loss of all the usual comforting guidelines. Going to college not only involves changing from the role of pupil to student, but also changing from one way of life to another which may be completely different in its ideals, morals and customs. Moving from one country to another, or from one time zone to another, are further examples of cultural transitions.

Where does depression fit into all this? Adventitious crises involving loss, bereavement and grief in the widest sense, will produce depression in individuals who cannot cope with the change, or in those who will ultimately cope, but in whom the depression appears before the adaptive mechanisms can be brought into play. Why should people get depressed in developmental crises? Why should certain periods of life be associated with depression more than others? These questions are not so easy to answer. Certainly, moving from one role to another, from one life stage to another, can be felt as 'leaving something precious behind' rather than as an exciting move into something new; there will be a depression arising out of the sense of loss. The challenge of the uncertainty of the future will evoke anxiety, giving a mixed picture of agitation. It may be that at certain stages of our development we are more vulnerable to external stress, and will show internal strain of which depression may be a part. This vulnerability can be based on genetic factors, individual weaknesses, biochemical and psychological changes. When change is taking place there is always room for something to go wrong. To be static may be safer, but then no growth will take place.

By looking at some developmental periods in detail it is possible to see how depression may express itself at these times.

In childhood

It used to be thought that children never got depressed because they did not show signs of depression which we can recognize in adults, but to understand a child's depression we have to see the world through the child's eyes. Children rarely say 'I feel depressed', but how many will have said, 'They seemed to forget that I was there' or 'They seemed to think I wasn't old enough to be involved or to understand'. From the child's viewpoint this is experienced as a denial of his or her own personal worth.

What more is needed to make a child feel depressed? A depressed child may not cry; he may become withdrawn, grow into himself and become silent or — the very opposite — he may become overactive or even violent, breaking up things, just as he feels 'broken up' inside himself. The studies made by René Spitz and others of the institutionalized child are studies in childhood depression. Much school refusal (school phobia) may be depressive, as well as being based on separation anxiety. Family studies have shown that the loss of a parent in critical stages of childhood, predisposes to overt depression in later adult life.

In adolescence

This is the bridging time between the dependence of childhood and the relative independence of adult life. Adolescents are characteristically moody, bad-tempered and depressed as well as wildly enthusiastic and uncontrollable. At a time when they are giving up the image of themselves as a child and forming for themselves a personal adult identity, it is not surprising that this should also be a time of depression, severe enough in some cases to lead to suicide. We have already mentioned the problems of being a student. This is a special category of adolescents who have particular problems and needs. All the pressures of developing sexuality, in conjunction with romantic idealism which is destined for disillusionment, lead to further depression. What has been anticipated in imagination as one of the greatest experiences in life, can turn out in reality to be something a great deal less, with

considerable resentment, doubt, guilt and disappointment. Depression is the result.

Engagement, marriage and childbirth are similarly liable to this contrast phenomenon. Around these important events are woven romantic fantasies fed by the tales of others, literature, TV, films and even a certain type of medical propaganda, so that anticipation is often far more enjoyable than the reality. Also, there can be a mourning for a lost freedom: the loss of being single with all its advantages, the loss of being 'just the two of us together' when the first child is born.

Keeping up with the Jones's enshrines the conflict of **middle age** where both men and women in their maturity may

feel challenged by the thrusting young who chase close behind. Many a middle-aged executive feels he cannot compete with the bright young men who are being groomed for promotion. Many a middle-aged woman feels at a sexual disadvantage to the more open sexuality of young girls. Depression can be a consequence for both.

Menopause, retirement and old age

Here there is a definite loss of function and loss of status. A woman cherishes her sexuality and the capacity to bear children; a man his power, represented by his earning capacity.

The middle-aged may feel that they are lagging behind — the retired and the old know that they are. The incidence of depression increases with advancing years, and tends to move from external to internal causes.

Depression is not inevitable at these critical stages of life, but clinical experience shows that it is those who have been through an early sense of loss in infancy, or have not had their needs met to some extent at that stage, who are more likely in later life to become depressed when change, external or internal, exposes them to stress. There is a re-experience of the early loss, and a re-enactment of the early depression.

CHAPTER 6
DEPRESSION AS AN ILLNESS

Depression A wife's story

'My husband is depressed. He has been depressed for about seven years. I try to make myself understand: I think about those awful, tense grey, pre-menstrual days when I drive along the road with my usual fear of accidents completely departed, because on those days I don't care if I am killed anyway. I tell myself that that is how he feels day in, day out. He is not depressed about anything. Some forms of depression are obviously normal and even healthy — as a response to bereavement, for example. My husband has an 'endogenous' depression, a depression 'growing from within' without any specific, identifiable cause.

Mornings are worst. He wakes very early, after sleeping fitfully, and is immediately overwhelmed with nameless forebodings and anxieties. He has almost always managed to get to work, where, by keeping going at top pressure all day, he is able to ward off a too great awareness of his troubles. By the time he comes home in the evening a complete change has taken place: he is fidgety, restless and has only a fleeting interest in anything. His boredom threshold is unbelievably low: for example, he cannot manage to read anything more than a newspaper headline, although he used to read widely.

He is desperate to have company but claims to find all our friends boring, and when I suggest inviting someone he turns down every name suggested. The restless fit is short-lived; within the hour he is asleep in the armchair and only rouses himself to stagger upstairs, sometimes as early as 8.30 and rarely after 10 pm. He works all day Saturdays. He dreads Sunday because there is no work to terminate the morning agony and it haunts him until dinner time, after which he goes upstairs and sleeps for two or three hours.

For him everything is monochrome: he cannot distinguish between good and bad, beautiful or ugly; he cannot make moral or aesthetic judgments or decisions. He feels remote and withdrawn and cannot allow himself to admit or express his emotions. He says he has never felt a single moment's happiness in his whole life.'

So far we have been looking at the kind of experiences which we all may have, and which, in given circumstances, can lead to depression in any of us; a depression as an adaptive response, or as an understandable shift of mood or of temperament. What, then, about depression in terms of illness?

When discussing whether depression was 'normal' or not, I defined illness in terms of the following three changes: a disturbance in the individual's normal functioning; a loss of efficiency as a result of this disturbance; and distress in the individual and those around him due to this loss of efficiency. I also indicated that the illness was made up, not only of the strain in the person concerned as a result of stress, but also of adaptive responses which the person makes to combat that strain. It will help to bear these basic concepts in mind as we go on to consider the ways in which depression can show itself as an illness.

As we do this we are moving into the so-called 'medical model' where a special vocabulary is used: **aetiology** is the understanding of the antecedent causes of an illness; **diagnosis** is the process of gathering all the evidence together, both **symptoms** (what the patient experiences) and **signs** (what the doctor observes), together with any tests which have been performed, thus coming to a conclusion about the type of illness which is present, and its relationship to other illnesses. **Prognosis** is forming an opinion as to the likely outcome of the illness: how long will it last, will it respond to treatment, will there be any recurrence, and will there be any long-lasting effects of the illness? Once we have arrived at an aetiology, diagnosis and prognosis, we can go on to a rational treatment or programme of **management.**

Causes of depression as an illness (aetiology)

For convenience, causes can be considered under three main headings — organic (physical), psychological and social — but, although convenient, this is an artificial division: what is physical in origin may well have psychological and social consequences, and vice versa.

Organic causes

Traumatic — following head injury and concussion; and certain operations, especially on particularly valued parts of the body such as the head, hands, eyes, ears, genital organs and so on.

Infective — particularly after influenza, but also infections such as encephalitis (brain fever) and hepatitis (inflammation of the liver).

Vascular — following a non-fatal stroke (haemorrhage) or thrombosis (blood clot) resulting in paralysis of a limb or loss of clear speech.

Hormonal — biochemical changes in the body such as those after childbirth (puerperal) or the change of life (menopausal), and when certain glands in the body fail as in the thyroid gland (myxoedema).

Epileptic — epilepsy does not always produce fits, but instead can result in unpredictable mood changes, or violent alterations of behaviour (psychomotor epilepsy).

Degenerative — as the brain ages, so it loses its efficiency. The person may be aware of this and become depressed as a result. Sometimes brains age prematurely and the person is said to be pre-senile. Old age can result in an irreversible loss of brain function, which is called dementia, and dementing patients often feel depressed.

Pharmacological — certain drugs prescribed to deal with other illnesses, in susceptible individuals can lead to depression, and the doctor has to be on the look out for this. It can happen with drugs given to control high blood pressure and with the use of certain types of contraceptive pill. It is important to stress that this is **not** inevitable but occurs in some susceptible individuals.

Our inherited characteristics, the handing on from one generation to the next of certain qualities and aptitudes, is contained in small packets called **genes** which occur in long chains or **chromosomes**. These are carried in our germinal cells — the sperm in the man and the ovum in the woman, which unite to grow into the new individual. Research by Eliot

Slater and his colleagues at the Maudsley Hospital, London, suggests that there is a gene for depression. This gene can be handed down from one generation to another and result in a predisposition to depression which may well be the basis of the susceptibility already described.

If we accept the genetical hypothesis, we still have to explain how the depression gene causes depression which involves turning to **biochemical** studies. It is reasonable to assume that depression is in some way related to the amount of activity in the brain. When people are depressed their reaction times are slowed down (provided there is no associated anxiety) which suggests that brain alertness and reactivity are reduced. Brain activity depends on the transmission of minute electrical impulses from one nerve cell to the next, and the transfer of energy across the gap between the cells is done by transmitter substances. These are known to belong to the group of chemicals called the **catecholamines.** These in turn are neutralized by other chemicals called **monamine oxidases.** The depressive gene could act either by increasing the monamine oxidases or decreasing the catecholamines. Certain antidepressant drugs used in the treatment of depression are called monamine oxidase inhibitors, and they act by knocking out the monamine oxidases, thus redressing the balance.

Other biochemical studies by Alec Coppen and his colleagues have shown that patients who have severe (and often recurring) depressions tend to accumulate more salt and water in their bodies than other patients who do not suffer from depression. Another clue is that some women get depressed in the week before menstruation starts (pre-menstrual syndrome), and this too is known to be due to retention of fluid which is corrected when the bleeding begins. The depression gene could also be active here by causing these changes in water and salt metabolism.

Psychological causes

Some of these have been discussed in detail already when we considered the early mother—child relationship and the responses in the child to the experience of separation and loss. In adult life, nearly all psychological causes for depression contain within them a re-creation of this early experience of loss. Some people are more prone to this than others and I have already suggested that it is those people who have not been able to deal adequately with this early loss who may be more prone to depression from psychological causes in later life.

Organic and psychological factors cannot be separated easily. If we look for depressive types, these susceptible people may have had this separation experience early in life or they may be of a certain body build (somatotype). It has been observed that people who are said to be of pyknic type, i.e. of average height but heavy build, especially around the shoulders and abdomen, tend to depression more than others. Is this psychological or is it physical? Could pyknic babies be more prone to loss or separation in some way? We do not know. Further, if we consider **compensation neurosis** — a condition in which, after some injury, the patient may be depressed or anxious to an extent quite out of keeping with the degree of the accident, and which may clear up completely after there has been a judicial settlement — we see the complex interaction of organic and psychological factors, especially if the original injury was to the head or brain.

Social causes

Are some social groups more prone to depression? Do certain social conditions make people prone to depression? Can the group cause certain of its members to become depressed? Do financial or climatic factors influence the onset of depression? Poverty, bad weather, minority-group membership, do not of themselves cause depression: there has to be some other factor or factors. Once more I believe the key lies in considering separation and loss. If poverty means a loss of status, if bad weather means the loss of some cherished plan, if being a minority-group member cuts you off from others and leads to persecution or loss of privilege, depression can result once more in susceptible individuals. Social factors also operate at critical periods of life and so can add to a predisposition to depression.

The one social factor which seems to correlate clearly with a tendency to depression is social isolation. A study by Hannah Gavron, a sociologist, into the lives of women held 'captive' in the home, showed that the women who were socially isolated, whether from upper or lower social classes, were the ones to get depressed. Studies by Peter Sainsbury into depression and suicide showed that the incidence of self-destructive acts was higher in those London boroughs where people were cut off from one another, whether they were wealthy or not. The isolated spinster, the widow or widower, were the ones more liable to end up killing themselves. Marriage, despite the other trials and tribulations it may bring, is less likely to cause suicide if not depression as such, because it avoids social isolation.

As an illustration of the complexity of the interaction of organic, psychological and social factors, let us take the example of a depressed middle-aged housewife.

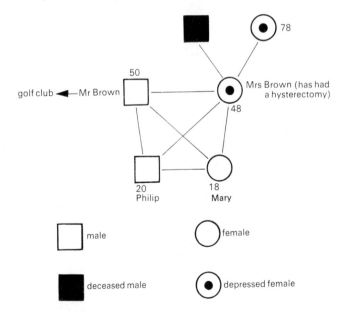

Family diagram (Mrs Brown)

Mrs Brown is forty-eight years old, married with two children. Her husband spends long hours at work during the week, and he goes out to the golf club at the weekend. She has not been well for some years and has recently had a hysterectomy (removal of the womb). The doctor believes that she also has myxoedema (sluggish thyroid gland). Her father is dead, but her old mother who has been depressed herself in the past, lives with the Browns and is difficult at times, especially at night when she wanders about the house. Mrs Brown is afraid that her mother may fall and break a leg. Her son, Philip, has done quite well at school but Mrs Brown doesn't like the company he is keeping; she also suspects that her daughter, Mary, may be sleeping with her boy-friend. She doesn't know definitely, but from things that have been said after a weekend when they went away together, she has her suspicions. She complains to her doctor among other things of being depressed. Now, let us look at the possible causes for her depression:

Organic factors

Her own mother's depression (depressive inheritance); myxoedema (hormonal change) and a hysterectomy (operation reaction).

Psychological factors

Her father's death (grief reaction); hysterectomy (loss of valued part of her body); conflict between the generations, with Mrs Brown caught up between her own mother on the one hand and her children on the other; anxiety about Philip and Mary and her own mother; fear that Mary may become pregnant or get venereal disease; and concern that Philip may get into bad habits through his friends.

Social factors

She is isolated, due to the absence of her husband at work during the day, and her husband and her children going away at weekends. She is attempting against increasing odds to keep up appearances for her husband's sake, and she has the pressures of trying to look after an elderly relative who is confused, particularly at night.

Mrs Brown is depressed, but who can say which of all these factors is the most important? How do they interact with each other? Which comes first? How important is it to make these distinctions anyway?

The diagnosis and classification of depressions

For a long time there has been argument about whether there are different types of depression, or only one depression which varies in intensity. Of course, this is considering depression as an illness and distinguishing depressive mood, depressive personality or experience. The 'unitarian' view held that there was only one form of depressive illness, but that it could vary in its form and intensity, depending on the circumstances that caused it and the kind of person who suffered from it. The 'dualist' view declined to accept this and claimed that there were at least two types of depression, basing the claim on clinical experience. It was maintained that there was a group of depressions to be called reactive depression, neurotic depression, exogenous depression, or justified depression — all

these names refer to variants of the one type. This type has certain clinical features and can occur at any age.

There was a second group of depressions to be called endogenous depression, psychotic depression or somatic depression. This tends to have different clinical features, and occurs later in life. The 'dualist' view became more complicated when experience suggested that some depression showed aspects of both reactive and endogenous depression. These were then called mixed depressions. Recent work in Newcastle, using computer techniques, confirms the 'dualist' view by showing that, when examined by factor analysis, clinical depressions tend to fall into two distinct groups which correspond reasonably well with the classical groupings, reactive—endogenous. It is also interesting to note that there was some overlap in the middle, corresponding to the group of mixed depressions.

There is some danger in calling certain depressions 'endogenous'. This implies that there is no known external cause and that whatever produces the depression must operate from within the individual. Clinical experience shows that nearly all so-called 'endogenous' depressions are triggered off by an external event, such as bereavement, infection, or disappointment, although the patient may not be aware of this and may believe that the depression 'came out of the blue' Another danger is that if you believe in endogenous

depression, you may be tempted to ignore external causes and so miss factors which could be used in the treatment or the prevention of a recurrence.

Contained within the reactive—endogenous dichotomy is an echo of Cartesian dualism. René Descartes, a seventeenth-century French philosopher, taught that man's mind was what separated him from the animal kingdom, and what distinguished one man from another. This led to an unfortunate schism in philosophy and opinion in general — man was thought of as having a body and a mind, separate and yet acting together. This is the historical basis for having physicians who care for the body and psychiatrists who care for the mind; having general hospitals and psychiatric hospitals. The psychosomatic concept of more recent years views man as a unity of body and mind (soma and psyche) in which body and mind are not separate but are aspects of each other. If that is so, then all depressions are, in a sense, both reactive and endogenous; they have both their psychological and their physical components.

In my own thinking I have tried to resolve the paradox and have settled, for the time being at least, for the following classification of depressive states:

Depressive reactions including depressive mood, depressive experience and depressive temperament. These I believe to be

largely psychologically determined, although expressed through the body. These can be **both** normal and abnormal.

Depressive illnesses which lie along a spectrum, at one end of which there is a predomonantly psychological causation and at the other there is a predominantly physical causation. **All** of these conditions are abnormal and pathological.

Abnormal depressive reactions come close to depressive illness at the psychological end of the spectrum, but differ from it in that the criteria for 'illness' are not present, i.e. the reaction may be deviant (abnormal) but it is not necessarily pathological. The person can still function and cope with his life.

Under the heading of depressive illnesses we can recognize the following: **manic-depressive psychosis** which is an illness characterized by alternating extreme excitement (mania), depression and a break with reality; **recurrent depressive illness** which may be a form of manic-depressive disorder in which only the depression shows through; **involutional melancholia** which is a form of agitated depression coming on in middle and late life, in rather rigid personalities; **senile depressions** which occur in. old age and are associated with ageing processes in the brain,

and **metabolic depressions** which are due to changes in body biochemistry, for example, puerperal depression after childbirth and menopausal depression at the change of life.

In making his **diagnosis** the doctor gathers together all the evidence before him and decides whether the depressive state falls into the category of depressive reactions or depressive illness and, if it is illness, to which sub-category it belongs. The clinical features may help to make this distinction clearer.

In **depressive reactions** there is nearly always associated anxiety as well as depression, so that the person feels tense and restless; he may have palpitations (an unpleasant thumping of his heart); he will lose his appetite and may have loose bowels (diarrhoea); at night his anxiety will keep him awake, or disturb his fitful sleep with unpleasant nightmares. His depressed mood is one of hopelessness and despair; he feels low in spirit and cannot summon up enthusiasm for anything. Even if he is enthusiastic, he cannot concentrate; instead he finds his mind wandering off to dwell on unpleasant thoughts of failure, rejection and despair. This mood is variable and at times he can be distracted from his depression by friends who encourage him 'to snap out of it' but, sooner or later, the despairing mood returns. There seems no point to life, no reason for going on. Often mixed with his anxiety and his depression are anger and resentment against a world which seems determined to be against him.

In **depressive illness** on the other hand, the characteristic feature is psychomotor retardation (the person is slowed up in mind and in body). His reactions are delayed and he cannot think properly, because his thought processes are so slow or because his head is empty. His body is slow: he moves as if in a dream; he does not avoid obstacles; his bowels are also slowed up, and he has constipation rather than diarrhoea. All his psychic energy has gone so he has no desire for sexual relations. This psychomotor retardation shows a tendency to improve as the day goes on, so that he feels worse first thing in the morning, but improves by lunchtime or teatime, only to feel bad again in the late evening and, again, first thing next morning. Characteristically, he may get off to sleep all right, but tends to wake in the small hours and be unable to get off to sleep again or just dozes fitfully. He will blame himself, rather than the world around him. He sees himself as full of guilt and self-reproach; it is his fault that he is like this, or it is due to some previously long-forgotten indiscretion. He may feel so bad in himself that he believes his body is actually rotting away. He hears voices criticizing him and sees people talking about him. He will feel so helpless, ashamed and guilt-ridden that suicide may seem the only way out.

CHAPTER 7
DEPRESSION AND SUICIDAL BEHAVIOUR

The subject of suicide is another book in its own right, but it needs considering briefly here because the suicidal person is so often depressed. The word 'suicide' means killing the self but, within suicidal behaviour, the motive of self-destruction is not always present or, if it is, it exists in varying degrees. Karl Menninger, an American psychiatrist, wrote that each suicidal person has the wish to die, the wish to kill and the wish to be killed. What he meant was that suicide is an aggressive act in which anger is directed both outwards against others and inwards against the self. Because of this mixed motivation, the contentious word suicide is best laid aside in favour of 'acts of self injury' which can be divided as:

a fully intended act — fatal, 'suicide'; or non-fatal, 'attempted suicide';
an act with other intentions — non-fatal, 'suicidal gesture'; or fatal, 'suicidal accident'.

In the first group the person is intent on his own destruction; in one event he kills himself, in the other he intends to do so but fails. In the second group the person is not intent on his own destruction as such, but is hitting back at others; in one event he draws attention to his situation and implies that he wants something done about it (appeal for help); in the other he does kill himself, but this is by accident — things have misfired.

In depressive reactions it is most common for suicidal gestures to occur (approximately 50,000 a year in England and Wales), but things may go wrong and an accident may happen. It is rare for a person who has a depressive reaction to kill himself outright unless the reaction is a very severe one. On the other hand, in depressive illness 'suicide' is common (over 5000 a year in England and Wales); it may fail at the last moment and be judged as 'an attempt'. These are not absolute rules: the risk has to be assessed in any given case. Suicidal gestures and accidents are most likely to happen with younger women of a hysterical or 'acting-out' personality. They are unable to clearly verbalize their internal conflicts and instead they convert their distress into actions which often have both an appealing and a manipulative element.

Suicidal acts and attempted suicides of self-destructive intent are more common among older people and more often men than women. The lonely, isolated old widower who has a chronic physical disability, such as a progressive deafness or chronic bronchitis, or who believes that no one wants him or that he is dying of cancer, is very likely to take his own life. Sometimes the intention is far from clear. Old, confused people may get up in the night to make a comforting cup of tea; they switch on the gas, turn away to look for the matches, get distracted by something else, forget what they were doing and, hours later, are found collapsed in a gas-filled room. Was it an accident, or was it suicide? Who is really able to know? Perhaps in all of these unhappy ends there is a complicated mixture of both.

If we examine suicidal behaviour in the setting of a developing progressive illness, the risk of self-destructive acts is higher at certain times than others. As a person becomes seriously depressed with marked ideas of guilt, self-reproach and despair, there is an increasing risk of suicidal intent. As the depression deepens, psychomotor retardation saps the mind of intent and the body of organization. Risk becomes paradoxically less because the severely depressed person cannot summon up enough will to set about his own destruction. Afterwards, under the influence of treatment, as the depression lessens and psychomotor retardation decreases, but while guilt (often masked) still exists, there is a secondary increase in the risk of suicidal behaviour. Many a family is caught out in this way; 'We thought he was getting so much better that we didn't feel we had to watch him so much. It was such a surprise that he did it then.'

It is in helping potentially suicidal people that the role of the volunteer comes into its own, with organizations like the Samaritans. With over 5000 deaths a year in this country, suicide prevention becomes very important, especially as the depression which underlies such self-destructive intent can be effectively treated.

CHAPTER 8
THE MANAGEMENT OF DEPRESSIVE ILLNESS

Just as the causes of depressive illness can be divided into organic, psychological and social groups, so management can be considered under the same headings. By 'management' we mean not only treatment in a very limited sense, but also caring for the total person in his total situation.

To begin as before with **organic or physical methods** of management, the basic principle is to deal with any underlying physical cause, such as an infection or biochemical defect, first, and to deal with the resulting depression in parallel.

Drugs

Tranquillizers and **sedatives** will be used if there is associated anxiety. **Antidepressants** are drugs designed to combat the physical basis of the depressive experience. They can be divided into two main groups: the **mood elevators**, such as the amphetamines; these raise the mood without dealing with the underlying change and thus are only palliative and, with the risk of drug misuse and drug dependence, are no longer widely used, as are the true **antidepressants** which alter the underlying biochemical change. They are again sub-divided into three groups: tricyclic antidepressants, such as Tofranil (Imipramine), tetracyclic antidepressants, such as Ludiomil (Maprotyline), and monamine oxidase inhibitors, such as Nardil (Phenylzine). Monoamine oxidase inhibitors have more dangerous side-effects, and so are less likely to be used nowadays. If there is marked insomnia drugs called **hypnotics** will be given to ensure a good night's rest. Finally, there is a drug called **Lithium**, which is a naturally occurring element. This substance, in the form of its salt (lithium carbonate), is believed to have a controlling effect on manic-depressive disorder by limiting the degree and the length of each mood swing and also may well reduce the chance of further relapses. It is a drug with side-effects and so its use has to be monitored carefully by frequent blood checks.

Electrical treatment

This kind of treatment is known as ECT (electro-convulsive therapy). It had long been known that people with epilepsy — a condition of naturally occurring convulsions or fits — often improved in mood after an attack; there is a kind of cathartic release and the patient feels 'lighter' in mood. In 1935 a Viennese psychiatrist, von Meduna, decided to try the effect of artificially induced fits on severely depressed patients and found that this form of treatment would dramatically halt the progress of an otherwise intractable and destructive depressive illness, which could go on untreated for as long as eighteen months if the patient did not kill himself in the meantime. The early methods used by von Meduna to induce fits in his patients were not without their own dangers and so two Italian physiologists, Cerletti and Bini, suggested that convulsions might be induced more gently and carefully by electrical means. The apprehension of the patient could further be reduced by the use of a quick-acting general anaesthetic and muscle relaxant. The modern form of this treatment is now a very sophisticated technique which, if given in proper circumstances by an experienced team of doctors and nurses, carries less risk than many other medical procedures to which patients are exposed.

Although the idea of ECT may sound frightening, the patient need not be distressed if it is done properly. Following each use of the treatment there may be some slight headache and loss of memory but these quickly pass off. After a course of some five or six treatments given twice a week, the patient often feels a dramatic release from his depression. Like all medical procedures, ECT is not a universal answer to depression, and is the subject of continuing controversy among different schools of psychiatry. There is agreement, however, that ECT must be selected for the correct patient if it is to be used at all and that it is more likely to be effective where there is a somatic component to the depression. This means that it is more likely to be effective in depressive illness than in depressive reaction, and particularly in depressive illness of the endogenous type. ECT can be given by itself or in conjunction with drugs.

While antidepressants may take up to three weeks before their effect is felt by the patient (they do not act immediately like aspirins), ECT can be given straight away to bring relief quickly, until the antidepressants take effect and continue the improvement in the long term.

Leucotomy

Leucotomy was a procedure discovered almost by accident, like so many medical advances. Doctors noticed that naturally occurring brain disease, or artificial brain damage following head injury, were often followed by a change in personality. Whereas before, the patient may have been tense, bitter and cantankerous, he became less worried, less inhibited and less concerned about himself.

In 1936 Egon Moniz, a neurosurgeon, decided to try to make controlled surgical lesions in the brains of severely depressed and severely anxious patients, with beneficial results. As with ECT, the early work had to be developed and made more sophisticated so that today, leucotomy, cutting the white fibres in the brain, is a very delicate and technical procedure. Again, like ECT, it is offered only to selected patients — those who have intractable depression with marked tension and self-destructive urges which has not responded to other treatments. Often, following a leucotomy, other treatments which previously were ineffective may become less so — the patient may begin to respond to drugs or ECT. Nevertheless the operation is now rare.

Hospitalization

This in its own right merits consideration in the management of depression. In the old days, psychiatric treatment was nearly always given in hospital since it was the only place in which such treatment was available. After the Second World War, out-patient clinics were set up and these offered an alternative setting for patient care but even so the out-patient clinics were often sited in, or close to the large mental hospitals.

Later, day care became a possibility, but it was the Mental Health Act of 1959 which emphasized community care. Now the doctor has a very real choice — 'Can I treat my patient at home, possibly using out-patient attendance or day care, or should I admit him to hospital?' There are a number of reasons for preferring hospital admission. The required treatment is only available there — ECT, leucotomy, group therapy and occupational therapy; continuing observation and assessment is required, since the patient may be suicidal and the family cannot give him all the support he needs; and it may help to get the patient out of his usual environment into a new one — a change of scene can be a tonic in itself, and can provide a setting in which new learning can take place.

Like all treatments, being in hospital has its disadvantages. It may encourage excessive dependence on the staff and lead to a passive reliance on them 'to get me better'. It often means living a considerable distance away from home, resulting in the patient losing contact with his home and local community. There is still some stigma attached to 'having been in one of those places'. Then again, hospitalization brings the patient into contact with severely disturbed people who may have a bad effect upon him. So the decision to admit someone to

hospital requires considerable judgement and experience, and should not be used in any sense as a routine method of treatment.

Psychological methods

These methods of management involve not only the use of psychological techniques as such, but also the bringing of the mind and feelings of one person into contact with the mind and feelings of another.

We are all capable of helping each other in this sense, but the difference between a good friend and a professional worker is the professional's ability to be both involved and objective at the same time. He is as much involved in the relationship as a good friend but, in addition, can stand back and see what is happening in objective terms — this is what an American psychiatrist, Harry Stack Sullivan has called 'participant observation'.

Counselling

This means helping the patient by joint examination of his problem; 'Let the two of us sit down and talk about your situation and see if, together, we may be able to discover what **you** can do about it.' Counselling involves finding out the facts

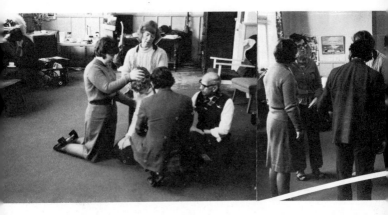

and determining what is really happening both at the level of reality and of fantasy. It also means gathering this information together in such a way that possible courses of action emerge. At times it means giving advice and making helpful suggestions, though this should always be done sparingly. Cynics will say that no one ever really asks for advice, only for confirmation of what he has already decided, but for the confirmation to be asked for at all indicates that there must be some doubt in the person's mind about whether what he has decided is the right course of action. Counselling also means giving emotional support while difficult decisions are being taken or are being acted upon.

Psychotherapy

This is a more specialized form of counselling which aims to promote new emotional learning. Psychotherapy has been called the provision of a 'corrective emotional experience'. The psychotherapy may be directed primarily at the unconscious aspects of the patient's life, or it may concentrate more on current events and attitudes. In terms of depression, psychotherapy is used to explore with the patient his inner conflicts which give rise to guilt and to aggression. It is concerned with looking at the original experience of loss in

childhood and seeing how this has been reactivated by recent events in the patient's life. In a sense, what happened 'there and then', helps us to understand and to deal with what happens 'here and now'. With the psychotherapist, the patient (hopefully) will come to understand his childhood abandonment experiences, not only in intellectual but also in emotional terms and, in the security of his relationship with the therapist, he will come to learn how to cope better with his current abandonment experiences.

Psychodrama

This is a new technique which is only just being developed in this country. The early Christian Church knew well that very complex ideas and feelings could only be expressed and understood in terms of drama: the medieval miracle plays not only educated the audience, but also caught the audience up in the action of the play, and it shared in the experience. Psychodrama uses the same techniques. As we act out being depressed, and the circumstances which have led to being depressed, we begin to feel and to experience ourselves and our situation in a way which only this technique can achieve. As we re-create lost experiences, we can get in touch with feelings that are locked up inside us, and we can make these

feelings 'work' on our behalf. We can share our depression with others, and they can share theirs with us, and in the process healing takes place. We can begin to bear what we can share.

Bringing others into the treatment situation takes us into the third area of management; **social methods**. In this context we are no longer concerned so much with what goes on deep inside a person, but with what goes on in his interactions with others. We are concerned with relationships in their usual social setting. Social intervention is infinite and cannot be enumerated in the same way as physical or psychological methods of management. Any way in which one individual helps another or makes aid available involves social interaction.

In the treatment of depression we are concerned with trying to modify the social environment of the individual so that there are fewer pressures on him and on his family, or so that he can make better use of his resources. The most frequent forms of social intervention will be things like financial help, improved housing, help with household management, finding better employment or training for specific jobs, introduction to social clubs and so on. The main agents of social care are local authority social workers or, possibly, the hospital-based social work team. They will be assisted by doctors, occupational therapists, employment

officers, probation officers, solicitors and so on. Social work is concerned with making scarce resources more equally available in the community and giving help and social support where it is most needed. The social worker is not some sort of benevolent fairy godmother, but rather an educator who helps people to widen their own horizons and to discover for themselves the resources they need.

Just as depressive illness is **caused** by a large variety of interacting factors, so **management** of depression must be carried out as a combined operation. To deal with only one cause and leave others untouched can hardly be called treatment in any sense of the word. Furthermore, when we treat an individual we are not thinking of him as an isolated machine which needs servicing, but as an interacting member of a social group.

Treatment for depression, if it is to be total in the sense of comprehensive, must involve all three approaches — physical, psychological and social. It is only when we deal with whole people in whole situations, that we are using treatment in the best sense.

It is also worth remembering that treatment is not a passive process; something which one person does to another, but a joint venture in which both the helpers and the helped are deeply involved.

CHAPTER 9
THE OUTCOME IN DEPRESSIVE ILLNESS

Determining the prognosis, or outlook, in an illness is one of the more difficult arts in medicine. At one level it may be little more than inspired guesses about what **may** happen; at another level it is a highly skilled exercise in the evaluation of probabilities. Events which are causally linked, which do not happen in random fashion, can be predicted according to the laws of chance and probability. These laws can be reduced to mathematical formulae and can be fed into computers to predict the probability of a given event happening with a high degree of accuracy. Currently, research is being done into the feasibility of using such techniques to identify 'high risk' and 'low risk' cases, that is to distinguish between those people who will get better anyway and those who need the maximum therapeutic intervention. As Francis Bacon, the philosopher, said, 'the office of medicine is to tune this curious harp of man's body, and reduce it to harmony. The physician hath no particular act demonstrative of his ability, but is judged most by the event; which is ever but as it is taken; for who can tell if a patient die or recover whether it be art or accident?'

Paradoxically, the advent of sophisticated treatment facilities like ECT and drugs have made it more difficult to predict the outcome of depression. Before such treatments were available the natural history of an illness could be studied. Depressive illness was found to have a characteristic beginning, course and end. The illness could last for anything up to eighteen months before recovery was complete and suicide could terminate the illness at any point. With any patient, the doctor could judge where he was in the course of his illness and predict, against the expected course, the likelihood of recovery. Now all that has gone. The timing of therapeutic intervention has altered the picture. If drugs are given too soon the depressive episode may not be able to be classified, and so prognosis will be difficult or even impossible. ECT brings the symptoms to an end, but has it necessarily influenced the underlying depressive process? A patient is put on drug treatment and gets better. Is this due to chance or has the drug really been instrumental in recovery? If we cannot establish this, we cannot say what the chances are of the drug stopping further relapses in the future. Again, to achieve a

good outcome, treatment intervention may be more appropriate and effective at one stage of the illness than another — as has already been described, the risk of suicide is certainly greater at one stage of the illness than another.

Despite this confusion, some general rules can be arrived at and it is said that generally a **better outlook** can be expected when: there is an obvious preceding cause for the depression; the patient is in one of the crisis periods of life; there is a rapid onset and a rapid build-up of the symptoms; and when the patient retains some insight, together with the wish to be helped.

The age of the patient, the family history and a history of previous depressions have a variable effect on outcome. Younger patients are more adaptable than older patients and thus cope better with depressive reactions. On the other hand, older patients may have an endogenous type of depression which will respond well to appropriate physical treatment. A positive family history of depression could be evidence of a general social and emotional vulnerability and therefore suggest a poorer outlook, or it could represent a clear-cut genetical inheritance leading to endogenous depression and a good response to physical treatment. Similarly, a history of previous depression in an individual patient carries the same mixed interpretation.

Arriving at a prognosis for a particular patient is an art, and general consideration can only give an indication of a tendency. The doctor has to take each case on its own merits, and has to weigh up all the pros and cons before he can finally say, 'Well, in my opinion, I think the likely outcome is going to be . . . .'

CHAPTER 10
MASKED DEPRESSION

When someone is depressed it is usually pretty obvious to those around him that he is not well; the mood of depression is often so 'catching' that other people, aware of their own reactions to him, can 'feel' that he is depressed. But depression **can** be masked, or hidden, in some way. Not everyone who **says** he is depressed is really suffering from a depression, and not everyone who **is** depressed is able to convey the fact either to himself or to those around him. So depression may go unrecognized, although the depressive process is still there causing distress to the sufferer and disrupting the lives of those around him.

Sir William Osler, the great Canadian physician, used to teach the students of his day the maxim 'know syphilis and all other things will be added unto you'. By this he meant syphilis was then a very common condition, but that it could announce its presence in uncommon ways so that the doctor would only be able to make the diagnosis if he kept the possibility of this widespread illness constantly in the back of his mind. Today, I think it is reasonable to paraphrase Osler and say 'know depression, and all other things will be added unto you'. Today it is depression which is the common condition that can show itself in uncommon ways.

Just think for a moment how easy it would be for you to go to your doctor and say 'Doctor, I am feeling depressed'.

To be able to do this requires you to recognize that depression exists as an entity and that it is what you are suffering from at the time. It means that you have to be 'in touch' with the inner world of your feelings and be able to assess these feelings and then translate them into words which you can then use to convey your experience clearly to others.

If you are **not** 'in touch' with your feelings and do **not** have the capacity or vocabulary to express them, you may go to your doctor and simply say, 'I just don't feel well; I've got bad nerves' and leave it to your doctor to determine what is wrong with you — to **tell** you that you are depressed. If the doctor is not 'in touch' with your feelings or does not appreciate vague complaints like the ones you are offering, he may not recognize that you are depressed and may diagnose something else like 'neurosis', 'nervous debility', 'hysteria' or whatever.

So the first and commonest cause of masked or unrecognized depression is the inability to recognize and express the depression.

What happens in dynamic terms when a person becomes depressed and his psyche, as it were, recognizes that this is so? All sorts of defensive mechanisms come into play of which displacement, conversion and denial are the commonest. How do these defence mechanisms operate?

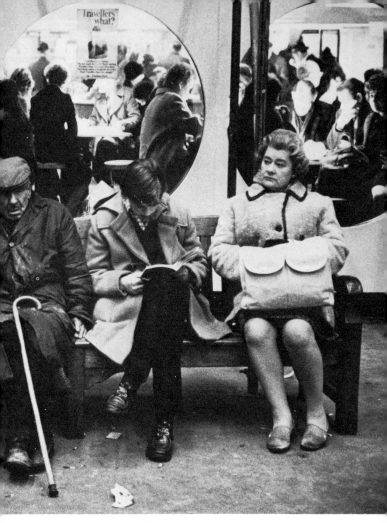

Displacement

This means that the person's attention is diverted from something which is threatening, on to something else which is less threatening and more easily acceptable. Attention and psychic energy become focused on to the less threatening object which can act as a smoke screen. When people become depressed, the depression itself may release so much anxiety that the original depression is lost — masked by the released emotion — so that the doctor diagnoses 'anxiety state' rather than 'depressive state'. Similarly, feelings of depression can be displaced or diverted into openly expressed irritability, resentment or anger. In the process once more, the original depression is lost sight of. False humour is used to cover up depression — the depression which lies behind the professional lives of so many people with reputations as clowns and comedians. The unhappy clown, on whom all the disasters of life fall, is a particularly pathetic figure and we react to him by laughing.

Conversion

With conversion, the psychic energy of the depressed state is not only diverted and displaced to be covered up by other feelings, but also, in a sense, it is converted into other experiences. Just as a seed is converted into the growing plant (the seed is not just covered over by the plant, but actually **becomes** the plant), so depression can become converted into bodily distress of which **pain** is the commonest expression.

Pain means that something is wrong, and that something is bad; psychological pain is converted into physical distress. Many patients find it easier to say to their doctors, 'I have a pain here (in the head, in the neck, in the back, in the stomach, in the chest) and I don't feel right', rather than to say 'I am depressed'. The physical accompaniments of the depressed state are perceived and experienced as pain or discomfort related to a particular part of the body. Often this relationship has symbolic nature: a neck pain may mean that someone is 'being a pain in the neck' to the patient, or people who are a 'headache' to us, cause us to have pain in the head. Depression related to childbearing is often linked with pain in the womb and so on. What the doctor has to do is detect what is happening, and to translate the symbolic expression of the pain in terms of its true origin.

The so-called 'converted depression' may not cause pain so much as a disturbance of function leading to a psychosomatic disorder. Various parts of the body cease to function properly — gastro-intestinal upsets perhaps, in extreme cases, lead to weight loss or enforced slimming (known as anorexia nervosa); respiratory upsets lead to asthma attacks or bronchitis. Breathlessness and pain in the chest during exertion suggest heart disease (remember the deaths from broken hearts after bereavement). Sexual disorders are common in depressed states and the patient will complain of impotence or loss of sexual arousal. Various skin disorders may appear; if someone has weeping eczema, it could be said that, symbolically, the skin is weeping for him. Repeated vomiting with no physical cause may suggest that the patient is having difficulty 'stomaching' something that depresses him. In all these examples the psychological distresses of the depressed state are converted into bodily disfunction and express themselves in body language (somatization). I must make the point here that we are only entitled to view patients in this way when all possible physical causes for the bodily disfunctions have been checked and found to be negative.

Denial

This means, quite simply, persuading oneself that something is not so in the hope that it will go away. If we tell ourselves that we are not depressed then perhaps the depression will go away. If we cannot see something, perhaps it is not there. Children play this game; they hide themselves from something unpleasant; they close their eyes and say, 'I can't see it, I can't hear it, so it's gone away.'

Many adults still have the emotional child inside them that plays up when things go wrong. Rather than facing up to depression and trying to determine its causes so that **perhaps** it can be dealt with, they would rather run away from it, turning their backs on it, denying its existence, believing that, in so doing, they are in fact making it disappear, making it go away.

The expression 'flight into health' has been used to explain this mechanism of denial. The phrase suggests that occasionally people who are ill, are so threatened by the fact of being ill that they try to persuade themselves and others that they are not ill at all; that they are quite healthy. In cases of depression, the patient may look happy (the so-called

'smiling depression'), he may even show evidence of
over-activity (of the hypomanic or excited kind), as if the over-
excitement were being used to deny the reality of the
underlying depression.

It is vital to be aware that depression can be masked so as
not to be taken in by the smiling depression, the
psychosomatic disorder, cases of pain, of anxiety and
excitement. It is easy to forget or fail to see the depression that
lies beneath the surface. At the opposite extreme, there is the
risk of seeing depression where none exists, but remembering
that depression is a fairly common human experience,
everyone should be less likely to miss it when it really does
exist.

CHAPTER 11
DEPRESSION, SEX AND ALCOHOL

At first sight it might seem strange to link depression with sex and alcohol — two facets of life which most of us associate with pleasure. It is this very expectation of pleasure which, if it is not forthcoming, leads to depression so easily.

Drinking and sexual activity are very closely linked together and not in the sense of plying someone with one in hope of the other! One of the first pleasures, tinged with a sexual overtone, which the baby experiences, is drinking his mother's milk. He feels warm and comforted, he feels good being close to the mother, he feels good being stroked and nursed by the mother and he invests this experience of drinking milk with the experience of goodness. Perhaps this association lies behind the proprietary names of some drinks — milk stout and cream sherries!

From another standpoint, when we are anxious about our capacity to meet the sexual demands of others, or when we are disappointed that they have not been able to meet our own, we often turn to alcohol for courage or for comfort. As has been said before, anxiety and disappointment are both closely linked with the experience of depression, so depression, sex and alcohol do not really make such strange bedfellows as at first sight.

Sex

What do we mean by sexuality anyway? Gender is the word used to define 'maleness' and 'femaleness' while sexuality is the word used to mean the full expression, both physical and psychological, of this gender role.

Our sexual lives are the basis of our existence. Freud claimed that it was the force of sexuality that drove the young baby to grasp out for his world and to explore it in detail — pressures which were essential for normal growth and development from receptive infancy through struggling adolescence to the maturity of adulthood. Sexuality is not just to do with sexual relationships and with procreation; in its essence it is the expression of our innermost and most personal being.

No wonder, then, that sex is so powerful, that sex makes

the world go round. But no wonder something so powerful and full of expectations is also the subject of failure and disappointment.

If a full, active and successful sexual life is synonymous with health and well-being, then anything which threatens sexual life will be powerfully associated with anxiety, and anything which leads to failure, whether in absolute or relative terms, will be associated with depression. Looking at it from another way, anything which reduces the inner confidence and energy which we hold in the centre of our being will affect our sexual performance. Anxiety and depression not only arise from poor sexual performance, they also contribute to it. This leads to the creation of a particularly vicious spiral.

Breaking into this spiral by looking at the way in which depression affects sexuality, it can be seen that any diminution of vital spirit will in turn reduce the store of sexual energy (libido) with resulting loss in sexual pleasure and sexual performance. Changes in an otherwise stable sexual relationship are often the first signs of a depressive disorder. Once there is this change in sexual behavior, there will be a secondary depression arising from the sense of loss of something which is valued, which further reduces sexual activity. The earliest changes are a falling off in sexual appetite and sexual energy. Then there is partial impotence in the case of the man or failure to reach orgasm in the case of the woman. Finally, there is total impotence with loss of erection and impossibility of ejaculation on the part of the man and frigidity or rejection of sexual contact on the part of the woman.

Some depressive personalities feel so under-valued (or so under-value themselves) that they cannot imagine themselves as valued sexual objects and so will shrink from sexual contact. If they make no sexual contact, they run no risk of rejection which would further reinforce the depression they feel. In addition, they feel that they do not want to risk disappointing a sexual partner and then be exposed to the resulting guilt. For them, having no sexual contact is reassuring and there are the women who talk of their menfolk as being 'golden husbands'; men who make no unreasonable sexual demands. On the male side there are the shy depressed men who keep to themselves and can only find sexual relief in escapist fantasy and the use of pornography.

Depression and sex are also linked in the opposite way. Some depressed people rush into a hectic sexual life, going from one partner to another, hoping desperately to find that 'ideal' person who will meet all their needs, who will make them feel '100 per cent'.

Sexual activity, like alcohol, can be used as a drug to cover up the desperation and the loneliness of being depressed. Young girls can go from one unsatisfying relationship to another, with all the attendant risks of illegitimate pregnancy or venereal disease. Older people get on to the marriage—divorce merry-go-round, pursuing an illusory 'perfect' partner who does not exist except in their imagination.

Alcohol

This has been used ever since Neolithic man discovered the intoxicant effects of fermented grain by accident. Here was release from the rigours of ordinary life, here was a liquid which relieved tension, assuaged grief, turned care into unconcern and gave release into happy oblivion. Men and women have been using it because of these properties ever since. Alcohol is a natural way out for the depressive; it may help him temporarily to forget, or help him to feel just that little bit better. However, inevitably comes the reckoning; after any release there tends to be a 'down' compensatory reaction — the glooms of the hangover, the guilts of the morning after.

Alcohol is a cerebral **inhibitor**, not a stimulant as is commonly believed. The relief of alcohol lies in its capacity to neutralize tension and anxiety. The good feeling comes from this release, this disinhibition. Alcohol 'takes the emotional brakes off' — **in vino veritas,** in wine there is truth. Alcohol loosens the tongue and releases desires, but, at the same time, can limit other capacities — hence the famous saying about alcohol: 'that it provoketh the desire, but taketh away the performance'. The depressive turns to alcohol for temporary release, but his problems are still there waiting for him. Continual misuse of alcohol in this way leads not only to destructive physical effects on the body, such as cirrhosis of the liver, but also to a psychological and physical dependence on the alcohol.

Any euphoriant will be grasped by a depressive as a potential antidote. Alcohol and sex are both experienced as euphoriants and therefore made use of by the depressive. The question is, 'Do they help?' As I have said, there are hidden dangers. Poor sexual performance with the attendant risk of rejection can confirm the depressive condition; excessive use of alcohol brings in its train problems often greater than the ones which it was used to 'drown' in the first place.

Finally, both alcohol and sex can be used as 'escapes' from reality. This may be satisfactory for short-term release but, however painful, ultimately we must return to reality in which the causes of our depression are rooted.

Perhaps the increasing drug bill in the National Health Service and the ever-growing demand for tranquillizers, pep-pills, antidepressants and hypnotics, reflect this same desire to escape from the pressures of the moment and to reach for a while a happier oblivion. But we do ourselves no service if we try to hide away from something which will not go away of its own accord, but which will only disappear if we are prepared to face up to it and struggle with it until we win through.

CHAPTER 12
CARING FOR THE DEPRESSED

ALL THE BEST PEOPLE HAVE HAD THEIR WORK REJECTED BY THEIR HOUSE JOURNAL AT SOME TIME OR OTHER..

CHARLES DICKENS... TOLSTOY... GALSWORTHY.. JANE AUSTEN.. BERNARD SHAW ...THE BRONTËS — ALL TURNED DOWN BY THEIR HOUSE JOURNALS.....

REALLY?

37%

WELL KNOWN FACT. FEELING BETTER? AGATHA CHRISTIE.... IAN FLEMING... DENNIS WHEATLEY..TENNESSEE WILLIAMS LESLIE CHARTERIS..P.G.WODEHOUSE....

What are the relative contributions to the care of depressed people that can be made by the professions (such as the family doctor) on the one hand, and by the volunteer or friend on the other? Although there is much in common, there are differences which are important and which, if they are not recognized, can lead to confusion, disappointment and frustration.

Exactly what is the role of the family doctor? He is the professional person that the family and the patient are most likely to turn to for help in the first instance. The family doctor, by virtue of his position in our society, is the doctor of first and continuing contact. Other professionals such as the social worker, or the psychiatrist may have episodic contact with the patient, but the family doctor is there in the background giving a sense of continuity to the patient and to his family. Further, as the title implies, he is the doctor of the family who should be in the best position to see the whole picture. He is less likely to consider members of the family in isolation, but should be able to see the problem on a broad canvas, spanning time as well as personalities. He will be aware of the social and cultural factors operating in his practice at the time and will know the economic pressures, the housing difficulties, the school problems, the lack of social amenities which put vulnerable people at risk.

For these reasons he is in a good position to be a coordinator of the help offered by other professionals or volunteers. He can make sure that there is no unnecessary overlapping, wastage or conflict of effort. He has a really vital role to play as someone who is close to the health of the family and who can distinguish as far as possible between physical factors on the one hand and psychological and social factors on the other. He can see where there is physical illness and take steps to put it right. All this is an important screening function which then leaves the psychiatrist and the social worker clear to operate within their own specialities and skills without constantly wondering whether some physical condition has been missed. A great deal of time can be taken up if either the social worker or the psychiatrist is encouraged by the patient to take on the role of family doctor and investigate physical factors and hunt out the cause of persisting physical symptoms. This practice is neither desirable nor does it come within the competence of the social worker or the psychiatrist.

Finally, within a psychological framework, the family doctor can make a diagnosis and start preliminary treatment. He can give simple support and encouragement. He can prescribe, if he wishes, antidepressants or tranquillizers, ensuring at least that the patient and the family get a good night's sleep. He can decide when referral to a specialist is necessary and, following such a referral, he will continue to be responsible for organizing and supplying the aftercare for the patient. Many depressions can be perfectly well treated in this way by the family doctor without any referral to a specialist.

In brief, then, the family doctor's job is to distinguish what is normal from what is abnormal; to distinguish what is abnormal **but containable**, from what is abnormal but not containable; and to initiate simple but effective care and to decide whether specialist care is necessary or not.

This is what doctors should do, but they do not all act in this way, whether they are family doctors or specialists. Not everyone has the same interest in, or the same sensitivity towards, the needs of the emotionally disturbed. Some doctors are better trained or have different experience from others. A family doctor may not always be able to measure up to the expectations people have of him — this applies equally to other professionals. This is why the work of professionals should be supported and complemented (hopefully) by the work of the volunteers.

The job of the volunteer or friend in the treatment of depression has been pioneered and developed by the Samaritan organization. The Samaritans are a group of ordinary people from all kinds of backgrounds who have chosen to offer help and friendship to those in emotional need. They are carefully selected and given a brief basic training. Throughout their work they have the support and backing of professional advisers. The strength of their organization lies in knowing their own limits and knowing clearly what they can offer which others cannot. They offer befriending and nothing else —

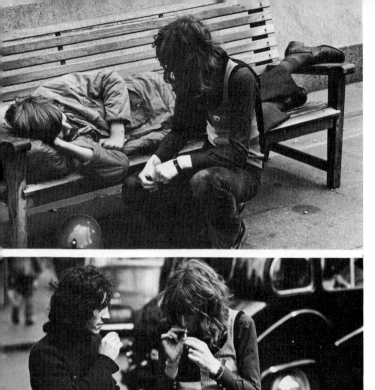

a listening ear in time of trouble. They agree to be available
by telephone or personal contact if asked by a 'client', but the
initiative lies with the client who has to **ask** for help. No one is
forcing help or contact on anyone. No one is taking an
authoritarian position, or is taking any formal action which
may lead to all sorts of consequences. Samaritans exist to offer
themselves — to offer a relationship.

This too is ideally the role of the friend, but not everyone is
cut out to be a Samaritan nor do they have the level of
self-control that is implicit in this kind of work. What, then,
can the friend across the street or over the garden fence **do**
when a neighbour is depressed? He can offer a relationship at a
time when a shoulder is needed to cry on, or a hand is needed
to hold for a time in what seems endless darkness. Depression
isolates people and simple contact with other human beings is
very helpful.

We can see one process of identification at work during this
contact-making. The befriender says, 'Yes, I have felt like that
too. I know what it's like to be depressed. You aren't alone in
feeling like this.' Support and encouragement easily follow,
but both have to be realistic and must not promise or imply a
depth of relationship which is neither intended nor is possible.
Simple distraction can help for a time but the danger here, if it
is used excessively, is that it can encourage denial of the
problem as has been described in connection with grief.
Offering a listening ear is more important than offering advice.
Offering companionship is more important than offering a
glib, ready answer to problems that may have no ready answer.
Some questions are by their very nature unanswerable. The
friend often plays a crucial role by encouraging a depressed
person to go and see a doctor when she is either afraid,
embarrassed, or too guilty to do so.

These are dangers to watch out for when helping a friend
who is depressed — don't try too much; let the person tell
you what is wrong in their own time and in their own way.
Don't take on too much; don't be tempted into getting
out of your depth. Offer simple help and stick to it. Don't
lose your objectivity; or get so close that you cannot
distinguish yourself and your problems, from those of the

person you are trying to help. Don't fall for the seductive response 'I feel that you are the only person who really understands me'. Perhaps you are, but the chances are that several other people have been told this too. Don't be flattered; hold on to reality. Offer what you feel you can give and then stick to it. Finally, don't be afraid to call in others; this is no reflection on you or the quality of your befriending. The really confident and able person knows when to go and ask for help; it is the ineffective helpers who get trapped into going out of their depth.

When you are a volunteer it helps to be in touch with others. There may be an organizer of voluntary service at your local hospital or clinic who will welcome your help and give your support in the work. There may be a branch of the Samaritans or MIND (National Association for Mental Health) in your own area. They organize conferences, and discussion groups: they can help with further reading and tell you what the next step for you may be.

It would be very unfortunate, if not disastrous, if people left the care of the depressed solely to the professional. There are not enough doctors, social workers and psychologists, to go round. Even if there were, the volunteer brings an additional dimension of caring. We must not be tempted to devalue what we can offer just because we are not professionals. Robert Burton, who in the seventeenth century wrote a book called **The Anatomie of Melancholie,** sums it all up very well when he says, 'If then our judgement be so depraved, our reason over-ruled, will precipitated that we cannot seek our own good or moderate ourselves, as in melancholie commonly it is, the best way for ease is to impart our misery to some friend, not to smother it up in our breast; for grief concealed strangles the soul; but when we shall but impart it to some discreet, trusting, loving friend, it is instantly removed for a friend's counsel is a charm, and it allays all our cares.'

CONCLUSION DEPRESSION AND THE SICK SOCIETY

In previous chapters I have been talking about the depression of a single person — albeit an individual viewed in the context of a relationship, or in a group setting, particularly the family. But can we ever talk of a **group** being depressed? Can we look for evidence of depression in the way in which a particular society behaves? Certainly we speak of a 'depressed economy', but we do not mean that an economy has feelings about itself, a consciousness of being depressed. When we talk of a 'sick society', of a depressed time in a particular group's history, we **do** imply a certain awareness of feeling in that society or group, not only by the individuals who go to make up the society or group, but also within the society or group as a whole.

Feelings certainly **can** be shared and experienced in a group. When one member is happy and the group can identify with that member, the whole group feels happy, such as at a wedding; likewise, if a member is sad or depressed, the group may tend to be sad or depressed. Are there parallels in the experience of the group that lead to depression, similar to those in an individual? Can a group feel deprived, can a group grieve over a bereavement? The answer is certainly 'Yes'. We talk of a group having a corporate identity so that the group assumes an identified unity in which all of its component members share. This group identity becomes analogous with individual identity and all the factors which I have described as causing an individual to feel depressed **can** apply to the group, except of course the purely medical individual factors like bodily disease. But, even in the group, certain medical factors can operate — when there is a lot of influenza about, a whole community can feel depressed and this depression is something over and above the simple aggregate of the individuals who may be depressed within the community.

How large can the group be and still show this group response? Basically, there has to be some sense of corporate identity. The group has to have a true sense of belonging together. The group can be a neighbourhood, a community, a tightly-knit part of the country like Tyneside or the Rhondda Valley, a whole nation even — provided there is this real sense of belonging together. People have to **feel** they belong together and are held together by invisible, but powerful, psychological and social links. In these circumstances the group can become depressed.

The depression may be a transient mood, like having just lost the Cup Final, or it may amount almost to an illness, a corrosive sickness, for example with the closure of the coal mines in an area where coal is the sole source of the economy. The depression can be a global experience like a nation losing its figure-head with the result that 'the nation is in mourning' — think of the USA after either of the Kennedy assassinations. The depression can be an attitude, or a way of life, as in the inherent depression of the deprived and under privileged racial minorities.

People speak of 'the sick society' but what does this really mean? Is it a literal statement or more of an analogy? Can a society be sick in the same way as an individual within it can be sick? The answer is 'No', in a literal medical sense but 'Yes' in a general, psychological and social sense. A whole society obviously does not have a corporate physical body, but it can have a corporate psychological mind and a corporate social conscience. When we talk of a sick society we therefore mean 'sick' in the sense of not functioning properly in psychological or social terms. Can we see evidence of this 'sickness'? When we are looking for psychological or social malfunction, there is more room for individual opinion about what is abnormal than there is in strictly medical terms. So people will differ in what they are prepared to interpret as evidence of a society's sickness, but there are social phenomena which are agreed to be evidence of 'something rotten in the State of Denmark' — a blind pursuit of material wealth for its own sake; a retreat into esoteric, religious cults and pseudo-faiths; an increased incidence of what are called 'catastrophic reactions'. Drug dependence, prostitution, gambling, violence, murder, suicide, warfare, 'self-poisoning' of all kinds, psychosomatic disorders, sexual perversions, and the breakdown of traditional values and rituals are all examples of this, and the decline and fall of the Roman Empire is historical evidence.

These sorts of factors are seen as evidence of a society in decline, a society characterized as depressed, dissatisfied, defeated and dropping out. Of course, depressed people see the world through depressive spectacles, so that in the end it may be the **observer** of the sick society who is depressed and sees it as such, rather than the society itself.

Perhaps, unless the Golden Age is a believable proposition, society always was 'sick' and always will be sick — in the sense of being disorganized, disordered and chaotic — but in its evolutionary history society may well have shown periods that have truly been more depressed than others.

Why are 'the old days' always seen as good, and the present always criticized as bad? Listen to Socrates on the youth of his day — 'Our youth loves luxury, has bad manners, disregards authority and has no respect whatsoever for age'; or an Egyptian priest in 2000 BC — 'Our world has reached a critical stage; children no longer listen to their parents; the end of the world cannot be far away'. Is it only a function of differential memory loss that we remember only good things in the past? We are always conscious of not only the good but also the bad of the present time. Is it a tendency in us to romanticize the past and to credit the historical with a glamour which it never had? In all of this we may be in danger, as in other situations, of over-generalization based on a particular instance. In any group, a person who is very influential may colour the whole group's mood by his own depression. In the same way one or two influential writers in a society may persuade the rest of us that the society too is sick and depressed when the depression and sickness, if there is any, lie in themselves rather than in what they observe. We must be careful not to generalize without good grounds for doing so.

It is easier to talk about the depression and sickness of others than about our own. It is easier to hide in the anonymity of the group than to make clear how one feels oneself. Thus there may be a danger of using glib phrases like 'a sick society' too readily as a smoke-screen behind which to hide our own grief and distress. Societies, like individuals, can be healthy and can be sick, but it is important to be wary of attributing to the **group**, feelings which really belong to ourselves as individuals — feelings which may, or may not, be shared by those around us.

Apart from these rather philosophical considerations, there is also implied in the phrase 'sick society' the idea that there is more illness around now than in previous eras. It is fashionable to think that modern men and women are exposed to particular stresses and strains in our modern world which were absent in earlier periods in history. We think of the shadow cast by atomic weapons and the reality of being able to totally destroy the environment in which we live; we think of the pressures of the mortgage payments or the so-called 'pace of life'. We think of all these things as being new and putting special strains on individuals and so imagine there must be more emotional disorder about. But is life really more stressful now than, say, in the eighteenth century? Take travel as an example. In going from Edinburgh to London today we may have to cope with the rush hours, the volume of traffic on the roads, getting to the airport on time and frustrating delays due to fog or road repairs. We may get all keyed up and tense and irritable and complain about the 'pace of life'. But in 1700 the journey would take several days in an uncomfortable coach with overnight stops in draughty inns; there would be muddy roads, highwaymen, pot holes, broken axles and the possibility of running into a plague area on the way. Life was pretty stressful then, just as it is now. Today we have the stresses of affluence; then there were the stresses of poverty and hardship. Today, wealth is a little more equally distributed in society; then wealth was the prerogative of the privileged minority. Contemporary records of the seventeenth and eighteenth centuries show that depression was well recognized; think of Hogarth's satire on the Rake's Progress and the squalor of the Debtors' Prison; suicide was just as commonplace then as it is now.

What has made a difference in our time is that we know more about what is going on; emotional disorders are recognized and people encouraged to come forward for help. In the seventeenth century there was a lot of hidden and private misery; in the twentieth century, distress and disaster take a common place in our lives through the mass communication media. Facilities for help are provided, so people come forward and the impression grows that there is more distress about, that we are truly living in a 'sicker' society.

It is medical history that improved methods of detection; for example, mass miniature radiography screening for tuberculosis or cancer of the lung, reveals more cases. It is not that there are more cases about; it is that they are being picked up more efficiently. During times of national disaster or wartime, it has been shown that the incidence of severe mental disorder, psychoses, remains about the same. and that neurotic disorders may even **decline.** During the troubles in Northern Ireland complaints of depression have been less even though times are hard. This is not just because people are too busy to complain but also, perhaps, because bitterness and resentment can be projected outwards on the 'enemy', rather than remain bottled up inside to create depression. It is not just that people only have time to notice the more severely disturbed, or that truly emotional tensions are decreased when there is a demonstrable external enemy; people group together for protection, there is a common goal and purpose, there is more social participation and less social isolation. In the Second World War many lonely and depressed people found friendship and purpose in London while they were sheltering in the underground stations during all-night bombing raids.

Depression has always been about; it is the cynics who feel that the doctrine of inevitable progress has been disproved and that there is much to feel despondent about today: the young are more decadent than they used to be, social morale is low, everyone is 'out for himself'. It is in this kind of mood — perhaps itself essentially depressive — that leads to the idea that we live in a sick society, a society that is sicker than it has ever been before. Yet 3000 years ago in Babylon, as inscriptions on clay pots clearly show, people were bewailing the standards of their society and despairing of there ever being a viable future.

Case histories

A student with depression

John is nineteen years old and is in his second year at university. He is having to study a subject that he is not very interested in, and has become involved with a group of disaffected students who rebel against everything. At first he felt happy to be with like-minded people, but then he begins to feel that he does not even belong to this group. He finds that he cannot compete with the more vigorous males and he begins to seek out the company of girls. He goes from one unsatisfactory relationship to another, but always comes back to one particular girl, he really wants her, but she seems to reject him every time because 'he does not satisfy her'. He neglects his studies and as a result fails his exams. There is talk of not letting him go on with his studies next term. He feels a failure at everything and takes an overdose of aspirin.

He feels that he has let everyone down including himself, and believes that he does not deserve to be helped. He seems sad but at the same time angry and resentful, and blames himself. He also blames others for not understanding him better, and almost challenges the doctor to get him better.

As he has not been sleeping at nights and has been becoming progressively introspective and moody he is given a sedative and encouraged to talk about himself and his feelings. In the beginning he does not find this easy, but he begins with confidence to discover aspects of himself of which he was previously unaware. Arrangements are made for him to return next academic term, and he attends the Student Counselling Service, seeing the doctor occasionally for review sessions. He resits his examinations and on this occasion does reasonably well. His relationship with his girl-friend improves, largely because he can now share with her some of his deeper feelings. The doctor feels that he will probably cope on his own now, and in some ways believes that John may become a stronger person as a result of this experience and his ability to come to terms with it.

A puerperal depression

Mary is twenty-two years old and has been married for eighteen months. She and her husband live on a council housing estate with a lot of other young couples. Her mother lives some three miles away and Mary keeps in regular touch with her, and her husband is beginning to complain about this. During her pregnancy with her first child Mary lost confidence in herself and was afraid of the labour that was to come. In due course she had her baby in hospital — a little girl of six pounds five ounces and all seemed well. Mary at this time is uncertain about her husband — she believes that he wanted a boy although now he protests that he likes his new daughter. Mary had some difficulty in breast-feeding the baby who is now on the bottle; Mary's mother keeps telling her that she should have persisted (she breast-fed all her babies). Mary has been back home now for some three weeks but she still feels weak and tired. The baby continues to cry by day and keeps them awake at night. She cannot seem to satisfy the child and she is becoming desperate at what she sees as her own lack of progress. Everyone keeps telling her to make an effort to cope better, but she does not know how to. She feels she is getting near the end of her tether. The climax comes one night when the baby won't feed but goes on crying. Mary hurls a soft toy at the baby and is horrified by a sudden impulse inside her to harm the child. She tries to tell her husband about this but he tells her 'not to be silly' and calls in the family doctor.

It is agreed that Mary and her baby should go into the local psychiatric unit because she does not seem to be able to cope with things at home. To complicate things the husband is not keen to ask his mother-in-law to step in because of the strained relationship between them. In hospital Mary and her baby are admitted to a mother and baby unit where she finds other young mothers with similar problems. She feels relieved to find that other mothers have similar problems to herself. She had thought that she must be going out of her mind to have

such dreadful feelings about her child. She is given a mild
sedative to help her to sleep at night and during the day learns
with others how to look after her child. In group therapy
sessions Mary discusses with the other mothers in a variety of
ways how young mothers can become isolated. She learns of
their uncertainty about their husbands and particularly about
the aggressive feelings which many young mothers have at this
time. Mary goes home on weekend leave and seems to cope
quite well. She is discharged from hospital having been there
for four weeks and arrangements are made for her and her
husband to visit the doctor for joint out-patient consultations.
These will be held once a week for some three to four weeks
and the doctor will then see them once a month for another
three or four months. The doctor feels that the outcome is
essentially good and Mary is encouraged that she is coping
better both with her baby and her husband.

A menopausal depression

Mrs Jones is fifty-three years old. She has been married for
twenty-eight years and has three children who are now
growing up and leaving home. She has always had 'trouble
with her periods' and dreaded coming to the change of life
because she had heard so many stories of how things can go
wrong, and she is not encouraged by the fact that her own
mother had a very bad time with her menopause. Mrs Jones
has had no periods now for some eighteen months and is
suffering from hot and cold flushes. She cannot concentrate
on her housework and takes little interest in what is happening
around her. She weeps at the slightest upset and her husband
gets exasperated with her and tells her 'to pull herself
together'. He is going through a particularly important time
with his business and feels that he has not the time to spend
on what he sees as his wife's hysterics. At his club he finds his
friends have had similar troubles with their wives and he is
strongly advised to take a firm line with her. When he tries this
Mrs Jones becomes very angry, saying that he does not care for
her and that he is more interested in his business than in her
and the family. Mr Jones denies this vigorously but still is

often away at weekend conferences. Mrs Jones becomes slower and more confused in herself; she feels that she can no longer go on and one day, when her husband is out, she drinks a bottle of sherry for courage and then takes half a bottle of aspirin. When Mr Jones comes home later he finds his wife lying on the bedroom floor and in a panic sends for an ambulance. Mrs Jones is taken to the local casualty department and after she has recovered from her overdose she is transferred to the psychiatric unit. There she remains slowed up and confused, feeling that life is not worth living and that she is a failure. She is given sedation and antidepressants and begins to improve for a time, but she relapses and her hot and cold flushes grow worse. A physician is called to see her who recommends some hormone treatment to correct the imbalance of her menopause. Again, she improves for a time, but relapses once more. The psychiatrist, together with a social worker, begins to have individual sessions with her and her husband. In these sessions each seems to blame the other and say that it is their fault for not trying. Joint counselling sessions are arranged and Mrs Jones goes home on long leave; she manages fairly well but her hot and cold flushes continue. Her hormone treatment has to be adjusted and the out-patient therapy sessions continued; she will probably do quite well eventually, once she is through her menopause and her body has made the adjustment, but Mr and Mrs Jones will have to make some adjustment to each other as people.

A depression in old age

Mrs Peters is an old lady of seventy-eight. Her husband died two years ago and she lives on her own in a small country cottage. Her married daughter lives ten miles away in the nearest village, but tries to keep in touch with her mother as much as she can. The local vicar has visited her fairly regularly but one day he is surprised to hear Mrs Peters claim that she has been an evil, wicked woman and that she does not deserve to live. He tries to argue with her but Mrs Peters says that God is punishing her for her sins and that her bowels have turned to stone. She believes that her whole body will turn to stone in due course and that everyone will see her as a dreadful warning against 'doing bad things'.

The vicar calls in the Social Services Department because Mrs Peters is refusing to feed herself and meals on wheels are arranged. The social worker consults with the family doctor who gives Mrs Peters an antidepressant, but this only seems to make her more confused. By arrangement Mrs Peters is seen by a local psychiatrist, he diagnoses senile depression and recommends another antidepressant together with a tranquillizer, but there is no improvement. Ultimately, he arranges for her to have outpatient ECT and after five treatments Mrs Peters is very much better and cannot understand 'what came over her'. Arrangements are being made by the Social Services Department for her to attend a day centre for old people, and although she is reluctant to go, she eventually agrees to give it a try. Although she is very much better, her daughter notes that Mrs Peters tends to feel lonely at times and weeps to herself, so the daughter is not sure how much better her mother really is. She is afraid that she will have a relapse and that she and her husband will have to have Mrs Peters to live with them. The doctor and the social worker warn the daughter that this may well happen, but in the meantime they will try to help her to live in her own cottage for as long as possible.

An agitated depression

Mr Kellaway is fifty-five and a successful company secretary. He has just had what he calls 'a nervous depression', which began three months ago when he found that he could not face his work and that everything was piling up on top of him. He was discovered one day by a junior colleague sitting shaking at his desk and staring at the blotting paper. People had seen for some time that he was not himself, but they had not wanted to interfere. Mr Kellaway was admitted to a psychiatric unit where agitated depression was diagnosed in an over-conscientious, obsessional personality. He did not respond to antidepressants alone and ultimately had six ECT treatments with good results.

The story emerged that he had always had to strive to be perfect because this was what his family expected of their eldest son. He had to try to be as good, if not better than his successful father and equally successful uncle. He was not particularly intelligent, but by hard work he had made as much of himself as he could, and had risen up through the ranks of his company until two years ago he had been made company secretary. He had doubts about being able to cope with the job but his ambitious wife had spurred him on. Whereas before he felt he was in a position equal to his capabilities, now he felt stretched beyond his capacity. He kept looking over his shoulder at the bright young executives whom he felt were only waiting for him to make a mistake so that they could topple him from his position. He began working late at night and taking his work home to complete at the weekends. He had literally run himself to a standstill. As he learned from the doctor, it was not just the pressure of work on him, but his own internal ceaseless drive to be perfect. In a sense it was he who had brought it all upon himself. Whether he will stay well in the future or not, will depend on how well he is able to compromise between doing what his position demands of him, and what his conscience forces him to do on top of his normal work requirements.

Depression in a woman with chronic pain

Mrs Andrews is fifty-eight years old. She has been attending her family doctor for years with progressive rheumatoid arthritis; this condition resulted in her wrists and knees becoming not only acutely painful, but also distorted with ugly swellings. In recent months her doctor has noticed that she is losing ground not only physically but mentally; she is looking older than her years and whereas in the past she always managed to smile despite her pain, she was now becoming listless and apathetic. She had been talking about not caring what happened to her and feeling that a life of continuous pain was not worth living. She was needing more and more pain-killers just to keep going. Recently she had hinted to her doctor that he might not have to go on treating her much longer, and he recognized this as a suicidal hint. The problem for him now is what more he can do for Mrs Andrews? He is giving her as many drugs as he feels he dare; if she has much more she will become dependent on them and suffer as much from their side-effects as from her arthritis.

One day he began telling her with frank honesty about his despair with regard to her condition, and his own uncertainty about what more he could do for her. Surprisingly, this seemed to help her a lot and gradually she has come to discuss her own feelings of guilt at not only being 'useless' to her family, but a burden to her doctor'. She and her doctor now know quite openly what lies in front of her, and she knows the limits of what he can do. This, instead of depressing her further, has in some ways helped her to become more confident and even hopeful. She feels that she and her doctor are working together on a problem, whereas before she felt she was making too big a demand not only on his time but on his sympathy. She now no longer talks of suicide and is content to have a regular fifteen-minute talk with her doctor every two weeks. At times she loses heart, but always seems to recover her strength and the determination to keep going.

Depression and personal inadequacy

Joyce Godfrey is thirty-six years old. She has been married for eighteen years to Fred Godfrey, a long-distance lorry driver, and they have four children, all still at school. Mrs Godfrey is a constant attender at her doctor's surgery. If it is not her sore back or her weak legs, one or other of her children has a cold, a cough, or catarrh; when Mrs Godfrey does not turn up at the surgery her doctor begins to wonder what is wrong. Recently she has been talking about being tired, run down and being depressed, and she certainly looks it. Everything that can go wrong seems to happen to her and her family, she cannot remember a time when she was not going to the doctor for a pill or a bottle of medicine. She remembers that her own mother used to do exactly the same. Her doctor has tried nearly all the antidepressants and tranquillizers available, but none of them work, so now he has referred her to the local psychiatric clinic.

The psychiatrist has asked for a social report which confirms a pattern of long-standing vulnerability and inadequacy. There are frequent rows between Joyce and Fred. He is never there when she really wants him and when he is at home, he gets angry with the noise the children make and either spends his time sleeping or down at the pub. Her children are all well known as trouble-makers at school, each one seemingly worse than the one before; the oldest boy Peter is on probation for petty theft and possessing drugs. Joyce cannot do anything right and every social agency seems to have been called into the Godfrey family at one time or another.

The psychiatrist realizes that this is not a depressive illness as such, but a depressive personality problem surrounded by social chaos. He gives Mrs Godfrey a new prescription not because it will do her any good, but because he recognizes her need to have something to lean on, even if it is a diagnosis of 'bad nerves' and a bottle of pills to go with it. She probably will not take the pills but having them prescribed for her is what matters. With the family doctor, the social worker, the probation officer, the head teacher, and the youth leader, the psychiatrist is trying to set up a supportive programme for the Godfreys and tries to coordinate the effort being put into this one problem family. He warns everyone that Mrs Godfrey will probably use the ploy of setting one worker off against another. The team of helpers will have to meet every so often to plan out their general strategies. Mrs Godfrey will continue to complain, but perhaps her doctors and the social workers will not feel quite so compelled to do what is impossible — that is cure her of her 'bad nerves', which are never cured as such: we just learn to live with them.

Hypochondriacal depression

Mr Stevenson is forty-five years old and is a tractor salesman. He does not look particularly ill but he always has a pain in his chest which goes down his arm when he exerts himself; he has been carefully examined in the general hospital and no cause for the pain has been found. All his tests, X-rays and cardiographs, are prefectly normal, yet he continues to complain of pain. A new family doctor comes to the practice and on going through Mr Stevenson's record he finds that he has consulted the practice over 200 times in the last ten years. What is interesting is that every complaint is of pain, but never pain in the same place twice and always in the absence of any significant illness. He has been up to the local hospital many times, so much so that his medical record folder is at bursting point with all the specialist reports. Each report says that nothing abnormal can be found and suggests referral to yet another specialist colleague. Apart from the gynaecologists and the paediatricians Mr Stevenson has been to see every specialist in the hospital, that is, except the psychiatrists. He has always refused to be referred there, saying that there was nothing the matter with him and that he wasn't mad. In desperation his family doctor has now referred him and Mr Stevenson has come defiantly to defeat yet another specialist.

There is such a contrast between the vehemence with which he declares that there is nothing wrong with him, and the persistence of his complaints of pain. What is this pain and where does it come from? It would be unkind to suggest to Mr Stevenson that he has no pain at all — that he only imagines that he has pain. Mrs Stevenson will confirm that at times her husband doubles up and his face goes white, the sweat standing out on his brow. Gradually it may be discovered that Mr Stevenson's pain is of psychological origin; he is suffering the pain of rejection and dejection. He was the youngest child of seven brothers and sisters and came as an 'afterthought'. No one ever had any time for him in the family. He was the sickly one of the bunch, and was always off school with a stomach pain or a headache. Having a pain was both a cry for recognition and a means of compelling interest and sympathy from others. Unfortunately now that he has grown up, he has alienated everyone's goodwill and has been labelled a hypochondriac. Mr Stevenson suffers from a long-standing depressive personality disorder and he will need a lot of patient understanding and help. The only question is whether he can make use of it, or is having a pain the only way in which this unfortunate man can ever make people listen to him and pay attention to him?

Further reading

Childhood depression

E. Erikson, *Childhood and Society,* Penguin, 1965.

D. W. Winnicott, *The Child, The Family and the Outside World,* Penguin, 1964.

Adolescence and depression

D. Miller, *The Age Between,* Cornmarket/Hutchinson, 1969.

The nature of depression

R. D. Laing, *The Divided Self,* Penguin, 1965.

Gordon Parker, *The Bonds of Depression,* Angus & Robertson, 1978.

Dorothy Rowe, *The Experience of Depression,* John Wiley, 1978.

C. Rycroft, *Anxiety and Neurosis,* Penguin, 1967.

A. Storr, *Human Aggression,* Penguin, 1970.

C. A. H. Watts, *Defeating Depression*, Thorsons, 1980.

Depression and suicide

K. Menninger, *Man Against Himself,* Hart Davies, 1938.

E. Stengel, *Suicide and Attempted Suicide,* Penguin, 1964.

Social factors and depression

E. Berne, *Games People Play,* Penguin, 1967.

G. Caplan, *An Approach to Community Mental Health,* Tavistock, 1961.

H. Gavron, *The Captive Wife,* Penguin, 1968.

Lord Taylor and S. Chave, *Mental Health and Environment,* Longman, 1964.

Medicine and depression

M. Balint, *The Doctor, His Patient and the Illness,* Pitman, 1964.

M. Hudson, *Doctors and Patients,* Hodder & Stoughton, 1967.

A. R. K. Mitchell, *Psychological Medicine in Family Practice,* Bailliere, Tindall & Cassell, 1971.

Index